PENGUIN TWENTIETH-CENTURY CLASSICS

THE ASSASSINATION BUREAU, LTD.

Jack London had a wild and colorful youth on the waterfront of San Francisco, his native city. Born in 1876, he left school at the age of fourteen and worked in a cannery. By the time he was sixteen he had been both an oyster pirate and a member of the Fish Patrol in San Francisco Bay, and he later wrote about his experiences in *The Cruise of the Dazzler* (1902) and *Tales of the Fish Patrol* (1905). In 1893 he joined a sealing cruise, which took him as far as Japan. Returning to the United States, he traveled throughout the country. He was determined to become a writer and read voraciously. After a brief period of study at the University of California he joined the Gold Rush to the Klondike in 1897. He returned to San Francisco the following year and began writing his fabulous Northland Saga. His short stories of the Yukon were initially published in the *Overland Monthly* (1898) and the *Atlantic Monthly* (1899); in 1900 his first collection, *The Son of the Wolf*, appeared, bringing him national fame. In 1902 he went to London, where he studied the slum conditions of the East End and wrote *The People of the Abyss* (1903). In 1904 he reported on the Russo-Japanese War for the Hearst papers; during the following year he traveled the lecture circuit, delivering lectures at Harvard and Yale. From 1907 to 1909, he sailed the South Seas, recording his adventures in *The Cruise of the Snark* (1911). From 1910 until his death he devoted most of his extraliterary energies to building his celebrated Beauty Ranch in the Valley of the Moon. An extraordinarily disciplined and prolific writer, during a career that lasted less than twenty years, he produced more than four hundred nonfiction works, two hundred stories, and twenty novels, including *The Call of the Wild* (1903), *The Sea-Wolf* (1904), *White Fang* (1906), *The Iron Heel* (1908), *Martin Eden* (1909), *Burning Daylight* (1910), *The Star Rover* (1915), and *The Little Lady of the Big House* (1916). After two extended visits to Hawaii, London died in 1916 at his home in Glen Ellen, California.

Donald E. Pease is Ted and Helen Geisel Professor of Humanities at Dartmouth College. He has written numerous books and articles on nineteenth- and twentieth-century American literature.

JACK LONDON

The Assassination Bureau, Ltd.

Completed by
ROBERT L. FISH
from Notes by
JACK LONDON

With an Introduction by
DONALD E. PEASE

PENGUIN BOOKS

PENGUIN BOOKS
Published by the Penguin Group
Penguin Books USA Inc., 375 Hudson Street,
New York, New York 10014, U.S.A.
Penguin Books Ltd, 27 Wrights Lane,
London W8 5TZ, England
Penguin Books Australia Ltd, Ringwood,
Victoria, Australia
Penguin Books Canada Ltd, 10 Alcorn Avenue,
Toronto, Ontario, Canada M4V 3B2
Penguin Books (N.Z.) Ltd, 182–190 Wairau Road,
Auckland 10, New Zealand

Penguin Books Ltd, Registered Offices:
Harmondsworth, Middlesex, England

First published in the United States of America
by McGraw-Hill Book Company, Inc., 1963
Published in Penguin Books 1978
This edition with an Introduction by Donald E. Pease
published in Penguin Books 1994

Library of Congress Cataloging in Publication Data
London, Jack, 1876–1916.
The Assassination Bureau, Ltd./Jack London; completed by Robert
L. Fish from notes by Jack London; with an introduction by Donald E. Pease.
p.   cm.
Originally published: New York: McGraw-Hill, 1963.
ISBN 0 14 01.8677 8
I. Fish, Robert L.   II. Title.
PS3523.O46A9   1994
813'.52—dc20   94-9213

Printed in the United States of America
Set in Bembo

CONTENTS

INTRODUCTION

Jack London owes his enduring literary reputation to the continued popularity of what Earle Labor has called his Northland Saga, a body of fictional and nonfictional writings about his experiences during the 1897 Klondike Gold Rush. But London's literary career had in fact begun four years earlier with the publication in the *San Francisco Morning Call* of "Story of a Typhoon Off the Coast of Japan," for which he was awarded that paper's top literary prize of twenty-five dollars. The art of the story lay in the subtle linkages London established between the violent forces released during the storm and the instinctual energies the crew mobilized in defense. From this first story London understood his literary craft to entail the disciplined recording of intense forces that in surging through him had precipitated an increasingly destructive urge to write. London found in the incitement to physical adventure an objective correlative for the excitement inherent to the writing drive. As he struggled to transmute the adventurer's immersion in experience into an equivalently absorbing field of force, London encountered anew the exhaustion he had experienced in his boyhood from work in a cannery. London's herculean work schedule (fifteen-hour workdays, up to forty-eight hours without food or sleep) finally required such an expenditure of physical energy that the conclusion of "Typhoon"—"And so with the storm passed away the bricklayer's soul"—might have also served as an eerie epitaph.

In the twenty-three years between the publication of "Typhoon" and his death from uremic poisoning at the age of forty, on November 22, 1916, London had produced nearly two hun-

dred short stories, twenty novels, and three full-length plays, along with several volumes of lectures and correspondence. *The Assassination Bureau, Ltd.,* the mystery thriller Robert L. Fish completed in 1963, was one of several of London's manuscripts published posthumously. When it appeared in the same year as John F. Kennedy's assassination, *The Assassination Bureau*'s central premise—that a shadow government of unelected officials was engaged in covert activities in the name of the national security —lent a weird aura of credibility to the manifold conspiracy theories that surfaced in the wake of that national tragedy.

If London had lived another fifty years, as did Robert Frost, who was born in 1874, two years before London, in all probability he could not have resisted adding to the still accumulating speculations about the events that took place in Dallas, Texas, on November 22, 1963. London's more than four hundred pieces of nonfiction certainly bear significant witness to his prodigious compulsion to have his say about almost any topic (from animal rights, anthropology, environmentalism, greed, Marxian socialism, Nietzschean supermen, political corruption, primitivism, prizefighting, racial oppression, social reform, and social Darwinism, to war and xenophobia) likely to incite impassioned debate.

Characteristically, London did not propose a systematic understanding of any of these topics, but approached each as if he were staking a claim on the energies the topic aroused. The restless curiosity with which London at first took possession of, then abruptly abandoned, controversial subjects paid tribute to the writer who had sought out these matters as occasions to exercise his craft rather than to accrue knowledge. London's essays are perhaps best understood as efforts at consuming these subjects with an appetite his rational processes could not possibly have gratified. Nevertheless, three of the cited topics—Marxian socialism, Nietzsche's doctrine of the Superman, and social Darwinism—in the contradictory responses they consistently evoked, provided London with a tendentious intellectual orientation.

In London's universe, altruism and individualism did not cancel each other out. Neither predisposition could be understood as either wholly itself or completely reducible to the other; each, instead, productively resisted the other. The aggression with which London pursued his socialist allegiances did not oppose but actively solicited his Nietzschean convictions. When configured' within the "evolutionary" narrative logic of social Darwinism, the Marxian socialist and the Nietzschean individualist became equally charged if mutually aversive alter egos. The intense energies released in their reciprocal animosity effected the extensive field of force through which London developed his other narrative characters, their plots and events.

The spectacular absence of motive for the instantaneous conversion of London's characters into their apparent opposites—the abrupt conversion within the first forty pages of *The Assassination Bureau, Ltd.*, for example, of Ivan Dragomiloff from a Nietzschean individualist into an apparently committed social reformer—derives in part from London's belief that these two figures constituted different valuations of the same social force. London had in fact lived the reversibility of these roles throughout his life. Having achieved at age fifteen a reputation as the most accomplished of the oyster pirates working the San Francisco Bay, London impulsively switched his loyalties. Within the span of a single year, London joined the California Fish Patrol in Benicia as a deputy patrolman assigned responsibility for the oyster pirates' capture. The writer would find metaphysical warrant for such reversals in the belief that the laws upon which the natural order depended for its perpetuation and the violence society was founded to oppose were, in fact, one.

London's susceptibility to the gold fever following the 1897 discovery of gold in the Klondike resulted in part from a wish to test this theory of symbolic violence. But the promise of attaining instant wealth on a barren, treacherous landscape also had profound appeal for his literary imagination. When he traveled to the Klondike, he was in search of subject matter that would

establish his literary reputation. Ironically the trip afforded London a reprieve from a writing compulsion whose pathology included a discipline that often left him with no time to eat or sleep. Before the Klondike expedition, London imposed immense demands on creative talents lacking an appropriate subject. When he returned to California in 1898, he numbered himself among the nineteen of twenty gold seekers who came out of the experience as impoverished as when they had entered it. But he had found materials that for the writer were more valuable than gold, rich veins of legend and folklore he would mine over the next two decades as the raw material for close to one hundred stories, essays, and lectures.

"It was in the Klondike that I found myself," London later explained. If that statement can be credited as true, the Klondike marked for his career a watershed of a still different kind. Jack London was born out of wedlock in San Francisco, California, on January 12, 1876. His mother, Flora Wellman, grew up as the black sheep in a relatively prosperous Ohio family; his father, "Professor" W. H. Chaney, was an astrologer, con artist, and philanderer who abandoned Flora shortly before Jack, who would never lay eyes on him, was born. When Jack was eight months old, Flora married John London, a widower and Civil War veteran with a carpenter's income and two daughters of his own. Along with her energy and craft Jack inherited from his mother an erratic temperament and a fatal attraction to "get-rich-quick" schemes that nearly bankrupted the London family during the boy's formative years but that his Klondike tales, in realizing, would install at the core of London's creative personality. The social standing that was afforded London the author provided as well the legitimacy denied him from birth.

London's teenage years might be characterized as a series of adaptations to increasingly turbulent circumstances. When he turned fourteen, Jack left school and worked to supplement the family income in Hickmott's Cannery for as many as eighteen hours a day at ten cents an hour. At fifteen he began what would

become a series of legendary careers when he bought the sloop *Razzle-Dazzle* and became known as "Prince of the Oyster Pirates" for raiding the commercial oyster beds in the bay off Oakland. Two years later he shipped aboard the *Sophia Sutherland*, a sailing schooner in search of seal furs in the Northwest Pacific, and scene of the events memorialized in "Story of a Typhoon Off the Coast of Japan." In 1893 he joined Kelly's Army, the Western regiment of Coxey's march on Washington, to protest the economic depression, then deserted in Hannibal, Missouri, on May 25, 1894, to tramp across the country. That adventure ended with his arrest for vagrancy in Niagara, New York, in late June, a thirty-day sentence in the Erie County Penitentiary, and the real-life basis for tramping reminiscences published thirteen years later in *The Road* (1907).

Following his twentieth birthday, London left Oakland High School without a diploma to start cramming for the University of California entrance exam. At the University of California at Berkeley, where he enrolled shortly thereafter, London joined the Socialist Labor party and discovered the passionate interest in Marxian socialism that led to the nickname "Oakland's Boy Socialist." He dropped out of Berkeley, after only one semester, to begin his formal career as a writer. He tried his hand at everything, writing not only scientific and sociological essays but short stories, humor, prose and poetry of every kind. "On occasion I composed steadily, day after day, for fifteen hours a day," London observed matter-of-factly. "At times I forgot to eat, or refused to tear myself away from my passionate outpouring in order to eat."

On July 25, 1897, six months after his twenty-first birthday, Jack London accompanied Captain J. H. Shepard on a four-hundred-mile trek across Alaska en route to the Yukon River, and a place to assuage his gargantuan appetites for writing matter. In the following passage from "Gold Hunters of the North" London described the literary substance found there as if it were imaginative matter whose exuberant self-display spontaneously

exceeded any writer's narrative powers. "The Alaskan gold hunter is proverbial," he remarked apropos of this drive, "not so much for his unveracity, as for his inability to tell the precise truth. In a country of exaggerations, he likewise is prone to hyperbolic descriptions of things actual. But when it came to Klondike he could not stretch the truth as fast as the truth stretched."

The Klondike encouraged London to find the nexus of contradictions informing his own character displaced onto an Arctic habitat whose conditions are generalized in the following description from "The White Silence": "All movement ceases, the sky clears, the heavens are as brass; the slightest whisper seems sacrilege, and man becomes timid, affrighted at the sound of his own voice. Sole specks of life journeying across the ghostly wastes of a dead world . . . Strange thoughts arise unsummoned, and the mystery of all things strives for utterance." Here, as well, law and violence were not opposed but encoded as interchangeable energies. London deciphered the code in "The Law of Life": "To perpetuate was the task of life, its law was death."

Throughout the stories collected in *The Son of the Wolf* (1900), the first volume of the Northland Saga, London proposed the Alaskan timber wolf as the representative in Nature of contradictions he believed socially pervasive. Like Jack London, the Klondike wolf found the (Nietzschean) loner and the (socialist) pack animal equivalently attractive social personae. The featured story of the volume contained an account of the elevation of the wolf into the white prospectors' totem animal. After "Scruff" Mackenzie sought to marry Zarinska, daughter of the chief of the Tananas, he aroused the jealousy of the tribal shaman. In his efforts to persuade Zarinska of Mackenzie's shortcomings, the shaman characterized the white man's malicious and destructive qualities as attributes inherited from the Wolf in contrast with "the creative principle as embodied in the Crow and the Raven." Scruff Mackenzie's rival thereby stigmatized him as the son of the Tananas' enemy clan. The name stuck. In the Northland tales written thereafter, Wolf became known as the tutelary

presence who guarded the entire white population, the figure in whose sign they conducted heterogeneous transactions ranging from fur trading to interracial marriage.

In an effort to correlate biological with literary paternity, Jack London married his former mathematics tutor, Bessie Maddern, on April 7, 1900, the same day Houghton Mifflin published *The Son of the Wolf*. Over the next three years, he became, in rapid succession, the father of two daughters, Joan and Bess London, the author of seven additional books, and the lover of Anna Strunsky. Strunsky was a brilliant young social philosopher of Russian-Jewish heritage London had met at socialist Austin Lewis's lecture at Stanford in December 1899, and with whom he later collaborated on a book-length dialogue about love, published anonymously in 1903 as *The Kempton-Wace Letters*. In that same marathon year London initiated a new love affair, this time with Clara Charmian Kittredge, the woman London believed was endowed with all the virtues of his "mate-woman." To mark this turning point in his public life, London published two books, *The People of the Abyss*, a sociological study of the abject living conditions in London's East End, and *The Call of the Wild*, a novella about a dog's success in adapting to the Klondike wilderness.

The Call of the Wild substituted track dogs for indigenous tribespeople as privileged mediators with the Klondike wolf, and London thereafter eliminated miscegenation as a narrative theme. The first tales in the Northland Saga were concerned with white prospectors whose struggles to learn the natives' ways led to the reciprocal commercial and social exchanges epitomized as interracial marriage. The shift in focus of *The Call of the Wild* represented a significant transformation in London's continuing narrative. In place of the gold hunters, London's narrative followed the tracks of a part Scotch shepherd, part Saint Bernard ranch dog named Buck, whose fortunes changed dramatically when a Mexican gardener kidnapped him from a Santa Clara estate.

The Call of the Wild replaced the earlier tales of miscegenation with this story of a mixed breed whose spectacular regression in the Yukon wilderness elevated him into London's literary trademark. This alteration in narrative focus reflected attitudes on questions of race and interracial marriage that prevailed among London's readers. As their means of taking verbal possession of the Klondike, Buck erased offending erotic relations from the readers' memory and offered in their place the sentimental education of a noble creature who always remained loyal to the masters to whom he truly belonged. The extensive relay Buck traced through the Northland wilds linked Judge Miller's Santa Clara estate with John Thornton's camp, and thereby expanded the circle of his masters' symbolic property to include the entire Klondike region. Thornton effectively incorporated Buck's instincts with his own brute impulses in a scene wherein, as proof of the claim that "nothing was too great for Buck to do when Thornton commanded," there appears the following astonishing description:

> . . . the men and dogs were sitting on the crest of a cliff which fell away, straight down, to naked bed-rock three hundred feet below. John Thornton was sitting near the edge, Buck at his shoulder. A thoughtless whim seized Thornton . . . "Jump Buck!" he commanded, sweeping his arm out over the chasm. The next instant he was grappling with Buck on the extreme edge. . . .

But London forged the most telling connection between Buck's former life as the central status symbol on Judge Miller's Santa Clara estate and his future destiny as the white totem for the region at the precise moment when the dog took revenge against the Yeehats, the native tribe responsible for the murder of John Thornton. "Death," London writes of Buck's inheritance of his master's self-destructive impulse,

left a great void in him, somewhat akin to hunger, but a void which ached and ached, and which food could not fill. At times, when he paused to contemplate the carcasses of the Yeehats, he forgot the pain of it; and at such times he was aware of a great pride in himself—a pride greater than any he had yet experienced. He had killed man, noblest game of all, and he had killed in the face of the law of the club and fang.

The totemic system London founded in the narrative of Buck might be understood as a linguistic compensation for Anna Strunsky's having unexpectedly broken off their interethnic relationship in September of 1902. But it is more simply an early indication of the racism that would eventuate in the notorious diatribes London directed in his subsequent writings against what he called the "yellow peril," and that would entail as an addendum to what has been called his "white logic" the proposition that he placed race loyalty above his obligations to international socialism. By 1903, U.S. imperialist ideology had mutated homegrown antiforeignism into a comparable strain of racism whose symptoms are discernible in the following observations from Henry Pratt Fairchild's *The Melting Pot Mistake*:

> What such a country really needs to concern itself about is the effect of race mixture. . . . If we can imagine the mating of two persons of absolutely pure stock of different races, each of the offspring would receive half of its determiners from the germ plasm of one race and the other half from the germ plasm of the other race. In other words, they would be strictly half-breeds . . . the mongrel.

London's contribution to U.S. imperialism now limited such experiments in breeding to his animal protagonists. The willingness the mongrel Buck displayed in *The Call of the Wild* to sacrifice his life in executing John Thornton's will would be

subsequently acted out on a much larger scale in the U.S. imperial adventure whose dates more or less coincided with Jack London's personal chronology, and whose trajectory—Hawaii, Panama, Cuba, the Pacific Rim—London's later tales would retrace. In *White Fang*, the sequel to *The Call of the Wild*, London redescribed the entirety of the Klondike as the narrative property of the gold prospectors who had depleted the region of its resources. Whereas *The Call of the Wild* had recorded Buck's regressive adaptation to the wilderness, *White Fang* reversed direction and described a wolf's transformation from a natural force into a surrogate national agent. White Fang's progression from Klondike nature to U.S. culture reenacted as its plot the nation's imperialist design.

The reversibility of the two plots mirrored a larger reversal at work in the ideological accounts of imperialism wherein the acquisitive drives of an imperial adventurer were transcribed as defensive reactions directed against what these adventurers described as the senseless aggression of native populations. By finding it thoroughly acted out in companion dog stories, London effectively reinscribed the entire circuit of U.S. imperial appropriation—its aggressive policies of colonial annexation followed by the blandishments of acculturation—upon the "white silence" of the Klondike. Delinking White Fang from the network of associations he shared with Northwest tribal communities, London realigned his interests with the more inclusive project of U.S. imperialism in the South Pacific, in which such later writings as *The Cruise of the Snark*, *South Sea Tales*, *The House of Pride and Other Tales of Hawaii*, and *The Son of the Sun* would play a significant role.

The dramatic shift in London's narrative attention from the kinship between wolves and men in the Klondike to the secret society of *The Assassination Bureau*, too, requires a more complicated explanation. Ivan Dragomiloff, the protagonist of London's unfinished novel, in fact had more in common with the patient Sigmund Freud named "Wolf Man" than with either the "Son

of the Wolf," his precursor in the London archive, or the were-wolf from the popular imagination.

I mention Freud's patient here as a point of historical reference and to provide a linkage between an obsessional theme in London's writing and a lifelong pathology. Jack London shared the Wolf Man's intense anxieties over the conditions of his parentage. The writer's intense fascination with wolves originated with the coincidence of two events: his reading of Rudyard Kipling's *The Jungle Book* and his discovery that he was William Chaney's illegitimate son. After reading the tale of a human child raised by wolves who instructed him in how to survive nobly in the wilderness, Jack London imagined himself a feral child for the remainder of his life. By way of this fantasy London defended himself against the images of violent dispossession—seven white wolves sitting outside his bedroom window—inhabiting the Wolf Man's dreams.

The Wolf Man shared the social space inhabited by were-wolves and feral children—the fabulous boundary separating nature from culture—but his nightmares disclosed a very different understanding of that boundary's effects. Stories of children raised by wolves fill in the missing link between humans and animals by transforming wolves into substitute parents. Legends of were-wolves reinstate that difference between nature and culture that wolf parents had traversed by disclosing the frightening consequences for the human form of parents who are actual wolves. The Wolf Man's anxieties do not refer to the inmixing of species but to the substitution of a violent for a humane environment. Freud referred to his patient Sergei Pankiev as the Wolf Man because of his recurrent fear that the seven white wolves sitting outside his bedroom window would swallow up his life.

While unlike in other respects, Sergei Pankiev and Ivan Dragomiloff shared a Russian past in which their patrimony was threatened (and in the case of Pankiev, finally lost) in the Russian Revolution. Dragomiloff played a minor part in the Russian Revolution of 1905 that had threatened to dispossess Sergei Pankiev of his patrimony, and Pankiev compulsively recalled the possible breakup of his family estate in the periodic return to his dream life of what Freud named a "primal scene." In this case the primal scene should be understood as a terrifying revelation of the bestial world that Pankiev associated with the Russian revolutionaries who threatened him with dispossession. After London's publication of *White Fang* and his beginning work on *The Assassination Bureau, Ltd.*, the wolf had become London's personal totem, a species of living property that, as had Buck for Judge Miller's possessions, established a taxonomy for his other writings (*The Sea-Wolf, White Fang*), as well as his real estate holdings ("Wolf House") and his second wife, Charmian Kittredge (London married "mate-woman" in 1905). But London's sole reference to wolves in *The Assassination Bureau, Ltd.*, was strictly metaphorical, and occurred when Ivan Dragomiloff nostalgically recalled his daughter Grunya's childhood incarnation as "a she-wolf of a cub without morality or manners."

In their migration from the "white silence" in London's Northland Saga to the white horror outside Sergei Pankiev's, London's totem animals had exchanged their furs for the uniforms of clandestine revolutionaries as well as the czar's secret police, who, in the interests of state security, routinely assassinated Russian dissidents. The Wolf Man's dreams dated back to the period of the Russo-Japanese War that Jack London covered for the Hearst syndicate, following his divorce from Bessie London in 1904. That same year, secret police sought out the czar's enemies in the vicinity of Sergei Pankiev's country estate. In the plot line of *The Assassination Bureau, Ltd.*, London rationalized the political murders the white wolves represented in the silence of Sergei Pankiev's dreams.

In response to a query from Winter Hall, his daughter's fiancé, Dragomiloff provided the following sketch of his life:

"My father was a contractor in the Russian-Turkish War. . . . He made a fortune of sixty million rubles, which I, as an only son, inherited. At university I became inoculated with radical ideas and joined the Young Russians. We were a pack of Utopianists and dreamers, and of course we got into trouble. I was in prison several times. My wife died of smallpox at the same time that her brother Sergius Constantine died of the same disease. This took place on my last estate. Our latest conspiracy had leaked, and this time it meant Siberia for me. My escape was simple. My brother-in-law, a pronounced conservative, was buried under my name, and I became Sergius Constantine. Grunya was a baby. I got out of the country easily enough, though what was left of my fortune fell into the hands of the officials. Here in New York, where Russian spies are more prevalent than you imagine, I maintained the fiction of my name."

This passage indicates Ivan Dragomiloff's capacity to impersonate both of the political agencies Pankiev feared—the secret police as well as clandestine revolutionaries—in a shadow government that predicted the KGB and the CIA, as well as the national security state. In his role as double agent, Ivan Dragomiloff also profoundly deepened Jack London's understanding of the relationship between violence and the modern nation-state.

The targets in *The Assassination Bureau, Ltd.*, differed from the Klondike wolves' prey in that they were not the victims of an explicitly acknowledged will to violence. Bureaucrats in Dragomiloff's agency favored covert activities and other substitutive procedures whereby the modern state concealed even from itself its necessary complicity with violence. In *The Call of the Wild*, London had rationalized Buck's violence against the Yeehats as the dog's "natural" response to their killing his master. But in *The Assassination Bureau, Ltd.*, London designated the state's authority to take the life of a private citizen as the most brutal exercise of violence. He then situated this authority in a bureaucratic organization founded by a Russian immigrant who exercised this power with the moral dignity and logical insight derived from wide reading in civil and moral law. That the assassins in Dragomiloff's Bureau could, without being seen or held accountable, take the lives of citizens, whose deaths they understood as the precondition for the recovery of a morally just society, indicates that, at least in the assassins' minds, they had not broken the law, but refined its efficiency.

Several trails link the subject matter in London's tales of the Northland with *The Assassination Bureau, Ltd.* A now-extinct land bridge once extended from Russia to North America and enabled the wolves from Sergei Pankiev's recurrent nightmare to roam throughout Jack London's Yukon. Two books published before London began working on *The Assassination Bureau, Ltd.*, in 1910 developed what might be understood as its transitional themes. In preparation for writing *The People of the Abyss* (1903), a sociological study of living conditions in East London, London reenacted Buck's regressive evolution. In August 1902 he disguised himself as a derelict in East London and then disappeared for six weeks into what were then believed to be the worst slums in the Western Hemisphere. In a letter to Anna Strunsky he vowed that as a consequence of this experience he would replace adventure with romance as his dominant genre: "I am made sick by this human hellhole called London Town. I find it almost impossible to believe that some of the horrible things I have seen are really so," London complained. "Henceforth I shall dream romances for other people and transmute them into bread and butter."

With the publication of *The Sea-Wolf* (1904) London complicated his resolve in a formula demonstrating uncanny intuition into the change in his public's needs. He did not abandon the theme of survival under abject conditions that had secured his popularity but interlinked it with motifs from the sentimental romance. "My idea is to take a cultured, refined, super-civilized man and woman," as he explained his new formula to his publisher, George P. Brett, "and throw them into a primitive sea environment where all is stress and struggle and life expresses itself simply, in terms of food and shelter." *The Sea-Wolf* and *The People of the Abyss* relocated Wolf, the totem figure from his literary imagination, in environments—the slums of London, the open sea—that, while different from the Klondike, nevertheless recalled its demands on the survival instinct. London's experiences in East London had confirmed his earlier conviction concerning the identity of cultural law and violence. Living under conditions in which a "dog-eat-dog" mentality supervened all other social relationships, London discovered a sociopolitical habitat of the lone wolf, whose literary formulation had been invented in *The Call of the Wild* and tested in Wolf Larsen, the protagonist of *The Sea-Wolf*. A literary precursor of Ivan Dragomiloff, Larsen combined instinctual courage with the ruthless will to power that constituted the only political order he ever acknowledged.

Following his marriage to Charmian Kittredge on November 19, 1905, London revised significantly the habit of construing his life only as raw material for his writing. In his eleven years of marriage to Charmian, the couple reversed this understanding and turned London's most popular literary formula—combining the themes of survival and sentimental romance—into the basis for their relationship. After they set sail in 1907 for a seven-year around-the-world cruise on *Snark*, the schooner London had had built for thirty-five thousand dollars, the theme of survival predominated. During extensive travel throughout the South Seas and Polynesia—from Hawaii to the Marquesas Islands, Tahiti, New Hebrides, Fiji, Solomon Islands, Australia—Jack and Charmian contracted multiple tropical diseases and returned after only two years to Beauty Ranch, London's California estate.

As Jack migrated from the region of the midnight sun to that of the rising sun, his stories registered more complex affiliations. His narrators' efforts at heroic self-possession intermingled with accounts of territorial annexation. In importing as national romance the illness, disappointment, and frustration he and Charmian had earlier exported to the South Sea islands, London constructed what might be considered an alternative economic system. His literary imports were as dependent on the success of U.S. imperialist policy in the South Seas as was S. Constantine & Co., the import/export business Ivan Dragomiloff used as a front in *The Assassination Bureau, Ltd.* After taking imaginative possession of the islands by appropriating their various cultural artifacts to the dominant themes in the national mythology, London invested the capital he had accrued from this symbolic property in an unsuccessful effort to make a killing in the California real estate market. While he was unable to capitalize on this investment during his lifetime, by the time of his death, in 1916, he had nevertheless accumulated more than a thousand acres of what would become the most valuable land in Sonoma County.

Although it included significant themes from London's preceding works, *The Assassination Bureau, Ltd.*, also introduced different sociopolitical materials. When London began work on the novel, the nation's twin demons of chauvinism and xenophobia had reemerged across the country. The Immigration Restriction League, an organization established in 1894, was representative of this influence. Its leaders addressed letters to governors throughout the United States and inquired ominously whether immigrants were desired in their states and, if so, of what races. The National League for the Protection of American Institutions, founded at about the same time, arranged conferences for the executive officers of "patriotic societies of the United States." The American Protective Association appealed to the interests of big business when it represented itself as a corporate organization able to consolidate Americans against what it referred to as "radical conspirators" and against foreign competition.

These "patriotic" societies had nominated the Mafia and the Molly Maguires, secret groups instituted in the late nineteenth century to protect the economic interests of Italian and Irish immigrants, as prominent examples of the anti-Americanism they were founded to combat. President McKinley's assassination by an anarchist in 1901 intensified a growing hysteria whose symptoms are evident in the heterogeneous attitudes that constellated around "aliens" in extant political tracts. According to this literature, immigrants were understood to be responsible all at once for (a) the nation's worsening socioeconomic condition as well as its political remedies; (b) heightened aspirations for self-improvement and the proliferation of subhuman urban environments; and (c) dramatically increased respect for law and order but also the terrifying rise in crime.

These ambivalent responses constitute the sociopolitical backdrop for incidents in *The Assassination Bureau, Ltd.* In crafting the novel, London did not isolate these contradictions or sort them into different characters and contrastive scenes but conscripted them into the service of a monumental plot reversal. After opening the narrative with a scrupulously detailed account of Dragomiloff's absolute commitment to the terms of agreement he had established with Will Hausmann, the secretary of the anarchistic Caroline Warfield group, only twenty pages later London constructed an encounter between Dragomiloff and another client, Winter Hall, during which Dragomiloff startlingly agreed to disband his entire organization. The terms of the dissolution required, moreover, that Dragomiloff himself become the chief target of the Assassination Bureau he had founded.

From its inception Dragomiloff's relation to the Bureau had been admittedly quite complicated. According to the Bureau's flow chart, he was primarily responsible for two separate company functions. As the Bureau's founder, he was chief executive in charge of issuing orders but also the adjudicative officer who decided on the ethical validity of agency contracts. His argument with Winter Hall effectively turned these two figures against each other. After deliberating on the grounds of their dispute, the judge in Ivan found the Bureau's chief executive guilty of a crime against the state, and issued the order that he be put to death. But the agency could not execute the order without also reenacting Ivan's crime. Marked as a target for an assassination he had himself ordered, Dragomiloff had effectively elided any practical difference between the Bureau's crime against the state and its usurpation of the state's absolute authority to execute criminals.

In his earlier transaction with Hausmann, Dragomiloff had carefully explained the ethical standards according to which the Bureau conducted such business. When Hausmann proposed the anarchist slogan "the hounds of the law must be taught the red lesson again" as the rationale for assassinating a corrupt chief of police, Dragomiloff refused this incendiary rhetoric as antithetical to the organization's two working rules: (1) the Bureau would not "fill an order" until Dragomiloff was satisfied that it was ethically justifiable; (2) if the Bureau failed to complete the assignment after one full year, the money would be returned, less ten percent for processing it. This account distinguished the Assassination Bureau's procedures from those of nativist groups and secret societies alike. The Bureau was unlike either of these social entities in that it could not be affiliated with any specific national, political, or ethnic cause, and its relatively open commercial transactions stood in stark contrast to the secret, ideologically motivated activities of nativists and nonnativists alike.

His organization originated, as Dragomiloff patiently explained the matter, for reasons that would be persuasive to anyone aware of the contradictions between the nation's juridical ideals and the actual judiciary processes, whereby the crimes of the powerful were concealed and the offenses of the powerless exaggerated. According to Dragomiloff, he had founded the Assassination Bureau to narrow this differential in the nation-state's distribution of justice. Hausmann's stipulation of motive for seeking the assistance of Dragomiloff's organization is interesting in this context for its complication of Dragomiloff's rationale. Following Dragomiloff's inquiring why Hausmann has not himself killed Police Chief McDuffy, the anarchist responds:

> "Also, I have a—er—a temperamental diffidence about the taking of life or the shedding of blood—that is, you know,

personally. It is repulsive to me. Theoretically I may know a killing to be just, but, actually, I cannot bring myself to do it."

The stark contrast between Dragomiloff's technically precise representations of the Bureau's procedures and Hausmann's emotional confession of his personal inability to carry out an assassination underscored still another of the agency's social functions. Too large to be visible to the untrained eye, the political assassinations carried out by Dragomiloff's bureaucracy are mediated by a long chain of command. When dispersed through the agency's flow chart, personal responsibility becomes an empty phrase enunciated in sentences that in corroborating a bureaucratic rationale apparently entail only procedural significance. Dragomiloff's bureaucratization of assassination had effectively reduced its political meaning to zero.

While Dragomiloff would altogether rescind a rational explanation for his actions, those actions nevertheless originated in an extremely rational debate. During an argument with Winter Hall, the young social reformer strongly opposed to the Bureau's activities, Dragomiloff proposed the opposition between the Nietzschean Superman who decided what was best for society and the social activist who believed in society's ability to reform itself, as the political contradiction the Bureau was founded to occlude. Dragomiloff "did not deny that he played the part of the man on horseback, who thought for society, decided for society, and drove society; but he did deny"—as London explained the basis for his dispute with Hall—"and emphatically, that society as a whole was able to manage itself." Following several days of intense intellectual argument, however, Dragomiloff conceded defeat to Winter Hall:

"I see, now, that I failed to lay sufficient stress on the social factors. The assassinations have not been so much intrinsically wrong as socially wrong. . . . As between individuals, they have not been wrong at all. But individuals are not individuals alone. They are parts of complexes of individuals. There was where I erred. It is dimly clear to me. I was not justified."

As a codicil to this stunning reversal, however, Dragomiloff designated the Assassination Bureau as the only social organization competent to destroy his agency, and thereby elevated Winter Hall's ethical arguments directed against the Bureau's political legitimacy into the precondition for a legally binding contract calling for Dragomiloff's assassination.

By way of this reversal, London restaged the central contradiction at work throughout his corpus. That Ivan Dragomiloff, the Bureau's founder, would not agree to his assassination without himself attempting to destroy the Assassination Bureau reveals the more inclusive structure of division we find underwriting all of London's tales; namely, their erasure of the differences between violent crime and the law. In dividing the founder of the Assassination Bureau into the two opposed roles of state criminal and his judge, London postulated the "Reason of State" as founded on the violence it was sworn to oppose.

In *The Assassination Bureau, Ltd.*, London's conflation of law and violence did not finally sort itself into a neatly resolvable contradiction but into the impossibility of choosing one or another of two absolutely opposed sets of affairs. In the following paragraph from *Man and Woman, War and Peace*, Anthony Wilden has provided a cogent analysis of this knot of contrariety that he refers to as a double bind.

A true double bind—or a situation set up, coerced, or perceived as one—requires a choice between (at least) two states of situations that are so equally valued and so equally insufficient that a self perpetuating oscillation is set off by any act of choice between them. A double bind is thus not a simple contradiction, but rather an oscillating contradiction resulting from the strange loop of a paradoxical injunction.

A true double bind was set up in the novel after Ivan Dragomiloff enjoined Winter Hall to hire the Assassination Bureau to "take out a contract" on its founder. Under a contractual obligation to associate himself with the Assassination Bureau he also wanted liquidated, Hall could not thereafter discriminate ethical from criminal activity.

London tightened the elements of this contradictory injunction into the social logic of the remainder of a narrative that, like the Bureau, was composed of characters and incidents in the service of an increasingly vertiginous implosive energy. In the romance between Dragomiloff's daughter, Grunya, and Winter Hall, London restored the theme of interethnic marriage; but without the promise of "development" that social Darwinism had guaranteed to London's previously invented characters, their relationship continually verged on disappearing into a void of mutual cancellation.

Overall, *The Assassination Bureau, Ltd.*, should be understood as having condensed London's two central themes—law and violence—into a singularly destructive social energy. As Winter Hall and the members of the Assassination Bureau pursued Ivan Dragomiloff from New York to Hawaii, the ensuing spectacle of his deferred capture is deprived of any rationale. As Ivan disposes of member after member of his agency, their deaths do not result in a reaffirmation of either democratic or socialist principles; they disclose the void at the core of political actions that are without goal or origin and refuse any justification other than their violent enactment. Every social space through which the principals enact this struggle becomes likewise reducible to the dimensions of a reciprocal annihilation. Something like the white silence that formed the ghastly backdrop of the Klondike tales subtends the actions represented here as well.

The usages into which each member of the Bureau, in rationalizing the Bureau's social purposes, had formerly invested his considerable intellectual energies could now, according to Breen, one of the Bureau's most intelligent agents, be found epitomized in an explosive device with which Breen intended to liquidate the agency. "Let me show you the quintessence of universal logic," Breen observed, "the irrefragable logic of the elements, the logic of chemistry, the logic of mechanics, and the logic of time, all indissolubly welded together into one of the prettiest devices ever mortal mind conceived." Like the components of this device, the Bureau's organization men could not align themselves with any political principle or social logic other than the irrefragable will to absolute violence that had incorporated them.

In turning this power against those who have presumed the authority to exercise it, however, London reveals a critically self-reflexive dimension of the novel disclosing London's ambivalent response to the imperial adventures that his other tales had naturalized. The ambivalence is evident in Dragomiloff's declaration of his new relationship to the agency:

> "Adventure. That is it. I have not had it since I was a boy, since I was a young Bakuninite in Russia dreaming my boyish dreams of universal human freedom. Since then what have I done? I have been a thinking machine. I have built up successful businesses. I have made a fortune. I have invented the Assassination Bureau and run it."

As subsequent events would make clear, the figure who interpreted his contract with Hall as an opportunity to initiate a deferred life of adventure was not Ivan Dragomiloff the founder of the Assassination Bureau, but his alter ego, Sergius Constantine. Constantine was the alias Dragomiloff used to found a business of another kind, S. Constantine & Co., the import company that, like Jack London's Beauty Ranch, was the chief beneficiary of the international commerce that U.S. imperialism had facilitated.

In signing the contract with Hall, Dragomiloff completes a change of identity from judge into fugitive by merging his interests in the Bureau with the commercial enterprise Constantine & Co., whose business ventures in Mexico, the West Indies, Panama, Ecuador, Tahiti, and Hawaii had already proved them appropriate sites for adventure. In tracking Ivan's efforts to elude his assassins, the narrative also reveals that trajectory as coincident with a circuit of territorial annexation where violence and governance had become likewise indistinguishable.

Perhaps it was London's increased ambivalence over his narrative's complicity with the rule of empire that led him to abandon the manuscript with the account of Breen's failed attempt to blow up the entire Bureau. While I cannot in the space of this Introduction do justice to the differences between the notes London left for the completion of his novel and the manuscript Robert L. Fish published, I nevertheless want to conclude with some brief remarks about the two texts that begin with an outline Fish uncovered among the London papers and included in an appendix to the 1963 version:

Hall loses Grunya, who saves Drago, and escapes with him. Then Hall, telegrams, traces them through Mexico, West Indies, Panama, Ecuador—cables big (5 times) sum to Drago, and starts in pursuit.

Arrives; finds them gone. Encounters Haas, and follows him. Sail on some windjammer for Australia. There loses Haas.

Himself, cabling, locates them as headed for Tahiti. Meets them in Tahiti. Marries Grunya. Appearance of Haas.

The three, Drago, Grunya and Hall (married) live in Tahiti until assassins arrive. Then Drago sneaks in cutter for Taiohae.

Drago assures others of his sanity; they're not even insane. They're stupid. They cannot understand the transvaluation of values he has achieved.

On a sandy islet, Dragomiloff manages to blow up the whole group except Haas who is too avidly clever. House mined.

Drago, in Nuka Island, village Taiohae, Marquesas. There is a wrecked cutter and assassin (Haas) is thrown up on beach where Melville escaped nearly a century earlier. While Drago is off exploring Typee Valley on this island, Hall and Grunya play off the assassin Haas, and think are rid of him.

Drago dies triumphantly: Weak, helpless, on Marquesas island, by accident of wreck is discovered by appointed slayer—Haas. Only by accident, however. "In truth I have outwitted organization." Slayer and he discuss way he is to die. Drago has a slow, painless poison. Agrees to take. Takes. Will be an hour in dying.

Drago: "Now, let us discuss the wrongness of the organization which must be disbanded."

Grunya and Hall arrive. Schooner lying on and off. They come ashore in whaleboat, in time for his end.

After all dead but Haas, Hall cleaned up the affairs of the Bureau. $117,000 was turned over to him. Stored books and furniture of Drago. Sent mute to be caretaker of the bungalow at Edge Moor.

The minor variations between London's notations and Fish's narrative testify to Fish's ingenuity, but a scene that Fish has added as the novel's penultimate chapter significantly altered London's central theme. In Chapter 18 of the Fish manuscript, Dragomiloff lures three of his assailants into a stretch of water between two Hawaiian islands that is known to the natives as

Huhu Kai—the "angry sea"—where a whirlpool draws them to their deaths. In adding this scene, Fish has not illuminated but simply replaced the following notation: "The three, Drago, Grunya and Hall (married) live in Tahiti until assassins arrive. Then Drago sneaks in cutter for Taionae. Drago assures others of his sanity; they're not even insane. They're stupid. They cannot understand the transvaluation of values he has achieved."

The "transvaluation" in Drago's values presumably had reference to his belated recognition that as the Bureau's founder he was exempt from the double binds incorporating its other members. In turning their efforts to assassinate him into gratuitous opportunities to demonstrate his prowess as an adventurer, Dragomiloff retroactively transmuted the entire agency (and the Reason of State it supplements) into an extension of his will to adventure. Unlike London, Fish refused to grant Dragomiloff a Nietzschean transvaluation and aspired to combine the assassin's absolute power over life and death with a freak natural occurrence. Fish attempted to reassign responsibility for the Bureau's liquidation to nature alone, but also to contain the escalation of violence within a *predictable* deviation from Nature's laws.

While it is difficult to ascertain his intention, Fish's revision may have been motivated by an aversive reaction to events in U.S. political history comparable to those which took place during London's lifetime. Fish completed the manuscript at the inaugural moment of an epoch of political violence that would take the lives of John and Robert Kennedy, Malcolm X, and Martin Luther King, Jr. These assassinations recalled the political murder of Archduke Francis Ferdinand of Austria-Hungary in 1914, which precipitated World War I. Whereas London's novel helped imagine World War I into existence, Fish's whirlpool isolated in Nature the violence that the Bureau's political assassinations had socialized.

With this revised conclusion, Fish had also rendered London's last novel formally symmetrical with "Story of a Typhoon Off the Coast of Japan," the tale with which London had begun his literary career. But the crucial difference between Fish's ending and London's does not refer to formal patterns. It entails a terrible knowledge about the violence endemic to the laws of the modern nation-state that Fish struggled to evade and that Jack London may have ultimately found more difficult to survive than any natural disaster.

—Donald E. Pease

SUGGESTIONS FOR
FURTHER READING

Books by Jack London

The Abysmal Brute. New York, 1913.

The Acorn Planter. New York, 1916.

Adventure. New York, 1911.

Before Adam. New York, 1907.

Burning Daylight. New York, 1910.

The Call of the Wild. New York, 1903.

Children of the Frost. New York, 1902.

The Cruise of the Dazzler. New York, 1902.

The Cruise of the Snark. New York, 1911.

A Daughter of the Snows. Philadelphia, 1902.

Dutch Courage and Other Stories. New York, 1922.

The Faith of Men. New York, 1904.

The Game. New York, 1905.

The God of His Fathers. New York, 1901.

Hearts of Three. New York, 1920.

The House of Pride and Other Tales of Hawaii. New York, 1912.

The Human Drift. New York, 1917.

The Iron Heel. New York, 1908.

Jerry of the Islands. New York, 1917.

John Barleycorn. New York, 1913.

The Little Lady of the Big House. New York, 1916.

Lost Face. New York, 1910.

Love of Life and Other Stories. New York, 1907.

Martin Eden. New York, 1909.

Michael, Brother of Jerry. New York, 1917.

Moon-Face and Other Stories. New York, 1906.

The Mutiny of the Elsinore. New York, 1914.

The Night-Born. New York, 1913.

On the Makaloa Mat. New York, 1919.

The People of the Abyss. New York, 1903.

The Red One. New York, 1918.

Revolution and Other Essays. New York, 1910.

The Road. New York, 1907.

The Scarlet Plague. New York, 1915.

Scorn of Women. New York, 1906.

The Sea-Wolf. New York, 1904.

Smoke Bellew. New York, 1912.

The Son of the Wolf. Boston, 1900.

The Son of the Sun. New York, 1912.

South Sea Tales. New York, 1911.

The Star Rover. New York, 1915.

The Strength of the Strong. New York, 1914.

Tales of the Fish Patrol. New York, 1905.

Theft: A Play in Four Acts. New York, 1910.

The Turtles of Tasman. New York, 1916.

The Valley of the Moon. New York, 1913.

War of the Classes. New York, 1905.

When God Laughs and Other Stories. New York, 1911.

White Fang. New York, 1906.

Books by Jack London and Others

London, Jack, and Strunsky, Anna. *The Kempton-Wace Letters.* New York, 1903.

London, Jack, completed by Robert L. Fish. *The Assassination Bureau, Ltd.* New York, 1963.

Criticism and Biography

Bridgewater, P. *Nietzsche in Anglosaxony: A Study of Nietzsche's Impact on English and American Literature.* Leicester, 1972.

Brown, D. *Soviet Attitudes Toward American Writing.* Princeton, New Jersey, 1962.

Foner, P. S. *Jack London: American Rebel.* New York, 1947.

Hendricks, K., and Shepard, I., eds. *Letters from Jack London.* New York, 1965.

Johnson, M. *Through the South Seas with Jack London.* New York, 1913.

Kingman, R. *A Pictorial Life of Jack London.* New York, 1979.

Labor, E. *Jack London.* New York, 1974.

London, C. K. *The Book of Jack London,* 2 vols. New York, 1921.

London, J. *Jack London and His Times: An Unconventional Biography.* Seattle, 1968.

Lundquist, James. *Jack London: Adventures, Ideas, and Fiction.* New York, 1987.

Lynn, K. S. *The Dream of Success.* Boston, 1955.

Ownby, R. W., ed. *Jack London: Essays in Criticism.* Layton, Utah, 1978.

Sinclair, A. *Jack. A Biography of Jack London.* New York, 1977.

Starr, Kevin. *Americans and the California Dream, 1850–1915.* New York, 1973.

Walcutt, C. C. *Jack London.* Minneapolis, 1966.

Walker, D. L., ed. *The Fiction of Jack London: A Chronological Bibliography.* El Paso, Texas, 1972.

————. *The Alien Worlds of Jack London.* Grand Rapids, Michigan, 1973.

Walker, F. *Jack London and the Klondike.* San Marino, California, 1966.

————. *The Seacoast of Bohemia: An Account of Early Carmel.* San Francisco, 1966.

Articles

Calder-Marshall, A. "Introduction." *Martin Eden* (The Bodley Head Jack London). 4 vols. London, 1965.

Etulain, R. "The Lives of Jack London." *Western American Literature* 11 (1976).

Geismar, M. "Jack London: The Short Cut." *Rebels and Ancestors: The American Novel, 1890–1915*. Boston, 1953.

Labor, Earl; Leitz, Robert; Shepard I. "Introduction." *Short Stories of Jack London*. New York, 1991.

Lachtman, H. "Criticism of Jack London: A Selected Checklist." *Modern Fiction Studies* 22, 1976.

Patee, F. L. "The Prophet of the Last Frontier." *Sidelights on American Literature*. New York, 1922.

Shivers, A. S. "The Romantic in Jack London." *Alaska Review* 1 (1963).

Walcutt, C. C. "Jack London: Blond Beasts and Supermen." *American Literary Naturalism: A Divided Stream*. Minneapolis, 1956.

Walker, F. "Jack London: *Martin Eden*." *The American Novel from James Fenimore Cooper to William Faulkner*, edited by W. Stegner. New York, 1965.

A NOTE ON THE TEXT

The plot of *The Assassination Bureau, Ltd.*, was included among fourteen brief story outlines Jack London purchased from Sinclair Lewis for seventy dollars on March 11, 1910. London wrote twenty thousand words and then abandoned the novel in late June of 1910, claiming he did not know how logically to conclude it. Robert L. Fish's completed version of the London manuscript was published in the fall of 1963 with London's "Notes for the Completion of the Book" and the "Ending as Outlined by Charmian London."

THE ASSASSINATION
BUREAU, LTD.

1

He was a handsome man, with large liquid-black eyes, an olive complexion that was laid upon a skin clear, clean, and of surpassing smoothness of texture, and with a mop of curly black hair that invited fondling—in short, the kind of a man that women like to look upon, and also, the kind of a man who is quite thoroughly aware of this insinuative quality of his looks. He was lean-waisted, muscular, and broad-shouldered, and about him was a certain bold, masculine swagger that was belied by the apprehensiveness in the glance he cast around the room and at the retreating servant who had shown him in. The fellow was a deaf mute—this he would have guessed, had he not been already aware of the fact, thanks to Lanigan's description of an earlier visit to this same apartment.

Once the door had closed on the servant's back, the visitor could scarcely refrain from shivering. Yet there was nothing in the place itself to excite such a feeling. It was a quiet, dignified room, lined with crowded bookshelves, with here and there an etching, and, in one place, a map-rack. Also against the wall was a big rack filled with railway timetables and steamship folders. Between the windows was a large, flattop desk, on which stood a telephone, and from which, on an extension, swung a typewriter. Everything was in scrupulous order and advertised a presiding genius that was the soul of system.

The books attracted the waiting man, and he ranged along the shelves, with a practiced eye skimming titles by whole rows at a time. Nor was there anything shivery in these solid-backed books. He noted especially Ibsen's Prose Dramas and Shaw's various plays and novels; editions de luxe of Wilde, Smollett, Fielding, Sterne, and the *Arabian Nights*; Lafargue's *Evolution of Property*, *The Students' Marx*, *Fabian Essays*, Brooks' *Economic Supremacy*, Dawson's *Bismarck and State Socialism*, Engels' *Origin of the Family*, Conant's *The United States in the Orient*, and John Mitchell's *Organized Labor*. Apart, and in the original Russian, were the works of Tolstoy, Gorky, Turgenev, Andreyev, Goncharov, and Dostoyevski.

The man strayed on to a library table, heaped with orderly piles of the current reviews and quarterlies, where, at one corner, were a dozen of the late novels. He pulled up an easy chair, stretched out his legs, lighted a cigarette, and glanced over these books. One, a slender, red-bound volume, caught his eyes. On the front cover a gaudy female rioted. He selected it, and read the title: *Four Weeks: A Loud Book*. As he opened it, a slight but sharp explosion occurred within its papers, accompanied by a flash of light and a puff of smoke. On the instant he was convulsed with terror. He fell back in the chair and sank down, arms and legs in the air, the book flying from his hands in about the same fashion a man would dispense with a snake he had unwittingly picked up. The visitor was badly shaken. His beautiful olive skin had turned a ghastly green, while his liquid-black eyes bulged with horror.

Then it was that the door to an inner apartment opened, and the presiding genius entered. A cold mirth was frosted on his countenance as he surveyed the abject fright of the other. Stooping, he picked up the book, spread it open, and exposed the toy-work mechanism that had exploded the paper cap.

"No wonder creatures like you are compelled to come to me," he sneered. "You terrorists are always a puzzle to me. Why is it that you are most fascinated by the very thing of which you are most afraid?" He was now gravely scornful. "Powder—that's it. If you had exploded that toy-pistol cap on your naked tongue it would have caused no more than a temporary inconvenience to your facilities of speaking and eating. Whom do you want to kill now?"

The speaker was a striking contrast to his visitor. So blond was he that it might well be described as washed-out blond. His eyes, veiled by the finest and most silken of lashes that were almost like an albino's, were the palest of pale blue. His head, partly bald, was thinly covered by a similar growth of fine and silky hair, almost snow-white so fairly white it was, yet untinctured by time. The mouth was firm and considerative, though not harsh, and the dome of forehead, broad and lofty, spoke eloquently of the brain behind. His English was painfully correct, the total and colorless absence of any accent almost constituting an accent in itself. Despite the crude practical joke he had just perpetrated, there was little humor in him. A grave and somber dignity, that hinted of scholarship, characterized him; while he emanated an atmosphere of complacency of power and seemed to suggest an altitude of philosophic calm far beyond fake books and toy-pistol caps. So elusive was his personality, his colorless coloring, and his almost lineless face, that there was no clew to his age, which might have been anywhere between thirty and fifty—or sixty. One felt that he was older than he looked.

"You are Ivan Dragomiloff?" the visitor asked.

"That is the name I am known by. It serves as well as any other—as well as Will Hausmann serves you. That is the name you were admitted under. I know you. You are secretary of the Caroline Warfield group. I have had dealings with it before. Lanigan represented you, I believe."

He paused, placed a black skullcap on his thin-thatched head, and sat down.

"No complaints, I hope," he added coldly.

"Oh, no, not at all," Hausmann hastened to assure him. "That other affair was entirely satisfactory. The only reason we had not been to you again was that we could not afford it. But now we want McDuffy, chief of police—"

"Yes, I know him," the other interrupted.

"He has been a brute, a beast," Hausmann hurried on with raising indignation. "He has martyred our cause again and again, deflowered our group of its choicest spirits. Despite the warnings we gave him, he deported Tawney, Cicerole, and Gluck. He has broken up our meetings repeatedly. His officers have clubbed and beaten us like cattle. It is due to him that four of our martyred brothers and sisters are now languishing in prison cells."

While he went on with the recital of grievances, Dragomiloff nodded his head gravely, as if keeping a running account.

"There is old Sanger, as pure and lofty a soul as ever breathed the polluted air of civilization, seventy-two years old, a patriarch, broken in health, dying inch by inch and serving out his ten years in Sing Sing in this land of the free. And for what?" he cried excitedly. Then his voice sank to hopeless emptiness as he feebly answered his own question. "For nothing."

"These hounds of the law must be taught the red lesson again. They cannot continue always to ill-treat us with impunity. McDuffy's officers gave perjured testimony on the witness stand. This we know. He has lived too long. The time has come. And he should have been dead long ere this, only we could not raise the money. But when we decided that assassination was cheaper than lawyer fees, we left our poor comrades to go unattended to their prison cells and accumulated the fund more quickly."

"You know it is our rule never to fill an order until we are satisfied that it is socially justifiable," Dragomiloff observed quietly.

"Surely," Hausmann attempted indignantly to interrupt.

"But in this case," Dragomiloff went on calmly and judicially, "there is little doubt but what your cause is just. The death of McDuffy would appear socially expedient and right. I know him and his deeds. I can assure you that on investigation I believe we are practically certain so to conclude. And now, the money."

"But if you do not find the death of McDuffy socially right?"

"The money will be returned to you, less ten percent to cover the cost of investigation. It is our custom."

Hausmann pulled a fat wallet from his pocket, and then hesitated.

"Is full payment necessary?"

"Surely you know our terms." There was mild reproof in Dragomiloff's voice.

"But I thought, I hoped—you know yourself we anarchists are poor people."

"And that is why I make you so cheap a rate. Ten thousand dollars is not too much for the killing of the chief of police of a great city. Believe me, it barely pays expenses. Private persons are charged much more, and merely for private persons at that. Were you a millionaire, instead of a poor struggling group, I should charge you fifty thousand at the very least for McDuffy. Besides, I am not entirely in this for my health."

"Heavens! What would you charge for a king!" the other cried.

"That depends. A king, say of England, would cost half a million. Little second- and third-rate kings come anywhere between seventy-five and a hundred thousand dollars."

"I had no idea they came so high," Hausmann muttered.

"That is why so few are killed. Then, too, you forget the heavy expenses of so perfect an organization as I have built up. Our mere traveling expenses are far larger than you imagine. My agents are numerous, and you don't think for a moment that they take their lives in their hands and kill for a song. And remember, these things we accomplish without any peril whatsoever to our clients. If you feel that Chief McDuffy's life is dear at ten thousand, let me ask if you rate your own at any less. Besides, you anarchists are poor operators. Whenever you try your hand you bungle it or get caught. Furthermore, you always insist on dynamite or infernal machines, which are extremely hazardous—"

"It is necessary that our executions be sensational and spectacular," Hausmann explained.

The Chief of the Assassination Bureau nodded his head.

"Yes, I understand. But that is not the point. It is such a stupid, gross way of killing that it is, as I said, extremely hazardous for our agents. Now, if your group will permit me to use, say, poison, I'll throw off ten percent; if an air-rifle, twenty-five percent."

"Impossible!" cried the anarchist. "It will not serve our end. Our killings must be red."

"In which case I can grant you no reduction. You are an American, are you not, Mr. Hausmann?"

"Yes; and American born—over in St. Joseph, Michigan."

"Why don't you kill McDuffy yourself and save your group the money?"

The anarchist blanched.

"No, no. Your service is too, too excellent, Mr. Dragomiloff. Also, I have a—er—a temperamental diffidence about the taking of life or the shedding of blood—that is, you know, personally. It is repulsive to me. Theoretically I may know a killing to be just, but, actually, I cannot bring myself to do it. I—I simply can't, that is all. I can't help it. I could not with my own hand harm a fly."

"Yet you belong to a violent group."

"I know it. My reason compels me to belong. I could not be satisfied to belong with the philosophic, nonresistant Tolstoians. I do not believe in turning the other cheek, as do those in the Martha Brown group, for instance. If I am struck, I must strike back—"

"Even if by proxy," Dragomiloff interrupted dryly.

Hausmann bowed.

"By proxy. If the flesh is weak, there is no other way. Here is the money."

As Dragomiloff counted it, Hausmann made a final effort for a bargain.

"Ten thousand dollars. You will find it correct. Take it, and remember that it represents devotion and sacrifice on the parts of many scores of comrades who could ill afford the heavy contributions we demand. Couldn't you—er—couldn't you throw in Inspector Morgan for full measure? He is another foul-hearted beast."

Dragomiloff shook his head.

"No; it can't be done. Your group already enjoys the biggest cut-rate we have ever accorded."

"A bomb, you know," the other urged. "You might get both of them with the same bomb."

"Which we shall be very careful not to do. Of course, we shall have to investigate Chief McDuffy. We demand a moral sanction for all our transactions. If we find that his death is not socially justifiable——"

"What becomes of the ten thousand?" Hausmann broke in anxiously.

"It is returned to you less ten percent for running expenses."

"And if you fail to kill him?"

"If, at the end of a year, we have failed, the money is returned to you, plus five percent interest on the same."

Dragomiloff, indicating that the interview was at an end, pressed a call-button and stood up. His example was followed by Hausmann, who took advantage of the delay in the servant's coming to ask him another question.

"But suppose you should die?—an accident, sickness, anything. I have no receipt for the money. It would be lost."

"All that is arranged. The head of my Chicago branch would immediately take charge, and would conduct everything until such time as the head of the San Francisco branch could arrive. An instance of that occurred only last year. You remember Burgess?"

"Which Burgess?"

"The railroad king. One of our men covered that, made the whole transaction and received the payment in advance, as usual.

Of course, my sanction was obtained. And then two things happened. Burgess was killed in a railroad accident, and our man died of pneumonia. Nevertheless, the money was returned. I saw to it personally, though it was not recoverable by law. Our long success shows our honorable dealing with our clients. Believe me, operating as we do outside the law, anything less than the strictest honesty would be fatal to us. Now concerning McDuffy—"

At this moment the servant entered, and Hausmann made a warning gesture for silence. Dragomiloff smiled.

"Can't hear a word," he said.

"But you rang for him just now. And, by Jove, he answered my ring at the door."

"A ring for him is a flash. Instead of a bell, an electric light is turned on. He has never heard a sound in his life. As long as he does not see your lips, he cannot understand what you say. And now, about McDuffy. Have you thought well about removing him? Remember, with us, an order once given is as good as accomplished. We cannot carry on our business otherwise. We have our rules, you know. Once the order goes forth it can never be withdrawn. Are you satisfied?"

"Quite." Hausmann paused at the door. "When may we hear news of—of activity?"

Dragomiloff considered a moment.

"Within a week. The investigation, in this case, is only formal. The operation itself is very simple. I have my men on the spot. Good day."

2

One afternoon, a week later, an electric cab waited in front of the great Russian importing house of S. Constantine & Co. It was three o'clock when Sergius Constantine himself emerged from the private office and was accompanied to the cab by the manager, to whom he was still giving instructions. Had Hausmann or Lanigan watched him enter the cab they would have recognized him immediately, but not by the name of Sergius Constantine. Had they been asked, and had they answered, they would have named him Ivan Dragomiloff.

For Ivan Dragomiloff it was who drove the cab south and crossed over into the teeming East Side. He stopped, once, to buy a paper from a gamin who was screaming "Extra!" Nor did he start again until he had read the headlines and brief text announcing another anarchist outrage in a neighboring city and the death of Chief McDuffy. As he laid the paper beside him and started on, there was an expression of calm pride on Constantine's face. The organization which he had built up worked, and worked with its customary smoothness. The investigation—in this case almost perfunctory—had been made, the order sent forth, and McDuffy was dead. He smiled slightly as he drew up before a modern apartment house which was placed on the edge of one of the most noisome East Side slums. The smile was at thought of the rejoicing there would be in the Caroline Warfield group—the terrorists who had not the courage to slay.

An elevator took Constantine to the top floor, and a push-button caused the door to be opened for him by a young woman who threw her arms around his neck, kissed him, and showered him with Russian diminutives of affection, and whom, in turn, he called Grunya.

They were very comfortable rooms into which he was taken —and remarkably comfortable and tasteful, even for a model apartment house in the East Side. Chastely simple, culture and wealth spoke in the furnishing and decoration. There were many shelves of books, a table littered with magazines, while a parlor grand filled the far end of the room. Grunya was a robust Russian blonde, but with all the color that her caller's blondness lacked.

"You should have telephoned," she chided, in English that was as without accent as his own. "I might have been out. You are so irregular I never know when to expect you."

Dropping the afternoon paper beside him, he lolled back among the cushions of the capacious window-seat.

"Now Grunya, dear, you mustn't begin by scolding," he said, looking at her with beaming fondness. "I'm not one of your submerged-tenth kindergarteners, nor am I going to let you order my actions, yea, even to the extent of being told when to wash my face or blow my nose. I came down on the chance of finding you in, but principally for the purpose of trying out my new cab. Will you come for a little run around?"

She shook her head.

"Not this afternoon. I expect a visitor at four."

"I'll make a note of it." He looked at his watch. "Also, I came to learn if you would come home the end of the week. Edge Moor is lonely without either of us."

"I was out three days ago," she pouted. "Grosset said you hadn't been there for a month."

"Too busy. But I'm going to loaf for a week now and read up. By the way, why was it necessary for Grosset to tell you I hadn't been there in a month, unless for the fact that you hadn't been there?"

"Busy, you inquisitor, busy, just like you." She bubbled with laughter, and, reaching over, caressed his hand.

"Will you come?"

"It's only Monday, now," she considered. "Yes; if—" She paused roguishly. "If I can bring a friend for the week end. You'll like him, I know."

"Oh, ho; it's a *him*, is it? One of your long-haired socialists, I suppose."

"No; a short-haired one. But you ought to know better, Uncle, dear, than to be repeating those comic-supplement jokes. I never saw a long-haired socialist in my life. Did you?"

"No; but I've seen them drink beer," he announced with conviction.

"Now you shall be punished." She picked up a cushion and advanced upon him menacingly. "As my kindergarteners say, 'I'm going to knock your block off.'—There! And there! And there!"

"Grunya! I protest!" he grunted and panted between blows. "It is unbecoming. It is disrespectful, to treat your mother's brother in such fashion. I'm getting old—"

"Pouf!" the lively Grunya shut him off, discarding the cushion. She picked up his hand and looked at the fingers. "To think I've seen those fingers tear a pack of cards in two and bend silver coins."

"They are past all that now. They . . . are quite feeble."

He let the members in question rest limply and flaccidly in her hand, and aroused her indignation again. She placed her hand on his biceps.

"Tense it," she commanded.

"I—I can't," he faltered. "—Oh! Ouch! There, that's the best I can do." A very weak effort indeed he made of it. "I've gone soft, you see—the breakdown of tissue due to advancing senility—"

"Tense it!" she cried, this time with a stamp of her foot.

Constantine surrendered and obeyed, and as the biceps swelled under her hand, a glow of admiration appeared in her face.

"Like iron," she murmured, "only it is living iron. It is wonderful. You are cruelly strong. I should die if you ever put the weight of your strength on me."

"You will remember," he answered, "and place it to my credit, that when you were a little thing, even when you were very naughty, I never spanked you."

"Ah, Uncle, but was not that because you had moral convictions against spanking?"

"True; but if ever those convictions were shaken, it was by you, and often enough when you were anywhere between three and six. Grunya, dear, I don't want to hurt your feelings, but truth compels me to say that at that period you were a barbarian, a savage, a cave-child, a jungle beast, a—a regular little devil, a she-wolf of a cub without morality or manners, a—"

But a cushion, raised and threatening, caused him to desist and to throw up his arms in arches of protection to his head.

" 'Ware!" he cried. "By your present actions the only difference I can note is that you are a full-grown cub. Twenty-two, eh? And feeling your strength—beginning to take it out on me. But it is not too late. The next time you attempt to trounce me, I *will* give you a spanking, even if you are a young lady, a fat young lady."

"Oh, you brute! I'm not!" She thrust out her arm. "Look at that. Feel it. That's muscle. I weigh one hundred and twenty-eight. Will you take it back?"

Again the cushion rose and fell upon him, and it was in the midst of struggling to defend himself, laughing and grunting, dodging and guarding with his arms, that a maid entered with a samovar and Grunya desisted in order to serve tea.

"One of your kindergarteners?" he queried, as the maid left the room.

Grunya nodded.

"She looks quite respectable," he commented. "Her face is actually clean."

"I refuse to let you make me excited over my settlement

work," she answered, with a smile and caress, as she passed him his tea. "I have been working out my individual evolution, that is all. You don't believe now what you did at twenty."

Constantine shook his head.

"Perhaps I am only a dreamer," he added wistfully.

"You have read and studied, and yet you have done nothing for social betterment. You have never raised your hand."

"I have never raised my hand," he echoed sadly, and, at the same moment, his glance falling on the headlines of the news-paper announcing McDuffy's death, he found himself forced to suppress the grin that writhed at his lips.

"It's the Russian character," Grunya cried. "—Study, micro-scopic inspection and introspection, everything but deeds and action. But I—" Her young voice lifted triumphantly. "I am of the new generation, the first American generation—"

"You were Russian born," he interpolated dryly.

"But American bred. I was only a babe. I have known no other land but this land of action. And yet, Uncle Sergius, you could have been such a power, if you'd only let business alone."

"Look at all that you do down here," he answered. "Don't forget, it is my business that enables you to perform your works. You see, I do good by . . ." He hesitated, and remembered Hausmann, the gentle-spirited terrorist. "I do good by proxy. That's it. You are my proxy."

"I know it, and it's horrid of me to say such things," she cried generously. "You've spoiled me. I never knew my father, so it is no treason for me to say I'm glad it was you that took my father's place. My father—no father—could have been so—so colossally kind."

And, instead of cushions, it was kisses this time she lavished on the colorless, thin-thatched blond gentleman with iron mus-cles who lolled on the window-seat.

"What is becoming of your anarchism?" he queried slyly, chiefly for the purpose of covering up the modest confusion and happiness her words had caused. "It looked for a while, several years ago, as if you were going to become a full-fledged Red, breathing death and destruction to all upholders of the social order."

"I—I did have leanings that way," she confessed reluctantly.

"Leanings!" he shouted. "You worried the life out of me trying to persuade me to give up my business and devote myself to the cause of humanity. And you spelled 'cause' all in capitals, if you will remember. Then you came down to this slum work—making terms with the enemy, in fact—patching up the poor wrecks of the system you despised—"

She raised a hand in protest.

"What else would you call it?" he demanded. "Your boys' clubs, your girls' clubs, your little mothers' clubs. Why, that day nursery you established for women workers! It only meant, by taking care of the children during work hours, that you more thoroughly enabled the employers to sweat the mothers."

"But I've outgrown the day-nursery scheme, Uncle; you know that."

Constantine nodded his head.

"And a few other things. You're getting real conservative—er, sort of socialistic. Not of such stuff are revolutionists made."

"I'm not so revolutionary, Uncle, dear. I'm growing up. Social development is slow and painful. There are no short cuts. Every step must be worked out. Oh, I'm still a philosophic anarchist. Every intelligent socialist is. But it seems more clear to me every day that the ideal freedom of a state of anarchy can only be obtained by going through the intervening stage of socialism."

"What is his name?" Constantine asked abruptly.

"Who?—What?" A warm flush of maiden blood rose in her cheeks.

Constantine quietly sipped his tea and waited.

Grunya recovered herself and looked at him earnestly for a moment.

"I'll tell you," she said, "on Saturday night, at Edge Moor. He—he is the short-haired one."

"The guest you are to bring?"

She nodded.

"I'll tell you no more till then."

"Do you . . . ?" he asked.

"I . . . I think so," she faltered.

"Has he spoken?"

"Yes . . . and no. He has such a way of taking things for granted. You wait until you meet him. You'll love him, Uncle Sergius, I know you will. And you'll respect his mind, too. He's . . . he's my visitor at four. Wait and meet him now. There's a dear, do, please."

But Uncle Sergius Constantine, alias Ivan Dragomiloff, looked at his watch and quickly stood up.

"No; bring him to Edge Moor Saturday, Grunya, and I'll do my best to like him. And I'll have more opportunity then than now. I'm going to loaf for a week. If it is as serious as it seems, have him stop the week."

"He's so busy," was her answer. "It was all I could do to persuade him for the week end."

"Business?"

"In a way. But not real business. He's not in business. He's rich, you know. Social-betterment business would best describe what keeps him busy. But you'll admire his mind, Uncle, and respect it, too."

"I hope so . . . for your sake, dear," were Constantine's last words, as they parted in an embrace at the door.

3

It was a very demure young woman who received Winter Hall a few minutes after her uncle's departure. Grunya was intensely serious as she served him tea and chatted with him—if chat it can be called, when the subject matter ranged from Gorky's last book and the latest news of the Russian Revolution to Hull House and the shirtwaist-makers' strike.

Winter Hall shook his head forbiddingly at her reconstructed ameliorative plans.

"Take Hull House," he said. "It was a point of illumination in the slum wilderness of Chicago. It is still a point of illumination and no more. The slum wilderness has grown, vastly grown. There is a far greater totality of vice and misery and degradation in Chicago today than was there when Hull House was founded. Then Hull House has failed, as have all the other ameliorative devices. You can't save a leaky boat with a bailer that throws out less water than rushes in."

"I know, I know," Grunya murmured sadly.

"Take the matter of inside rooms," Hall went on. "In New York City, at the close of the Civil War, there were sixty thousand inside rooms. Since then inside rooms have been continually crusaded against. Men, many of them, have devoted their lives to that very fight. Public-spirited citizens by thousands and tens of thousands have contributed their money and their approval. Whole blocks have been torn down and replaced by parks and playgrounds. It has been a great and terrible fight. And what is the result? Today, in the year 1911, there are over three hundred thousand inside rooms in New York City."

He shrugged his shoulders and sipped his tea.

"More and more do you make me see two things," Grunya confessed. "First, that liberty, unrestricted by man-made law, cannot be gained except by evolution through a stage of excessive man-made law that will well-nigh reduce us all to automatons—the socialistic stage, of course. But I, for one, would never care to live in the socialist state. It would be maddening."

"You prefer the splendid, wild, cruel beauty of our present commercial individualism?" he asked quietly.

"Almost I do. Almost I do. But the socialist state must come. I know that, because of the second thing I so clearly see, and that is the failure of amelioration to ameliorate." She broke off abruptly, favored him with a dazzling, cheerful smile, and announced, "But why should we be serious with the hot weather coming on? Why don't you leave town for a breath of air?"

"Why don't you?" he countered.

"Too busy."

"Same here." He paused, and his face seemed suddenly to become harsh and grim, as if reflecting some stern inner thought. "In fact, I have never been busier in my life, and never so near accomplishing something big."

"But you will run up for the week end and meet my uncle?" she demanded impulsively. "He was here just a few minutes ago. He wants to make it a—a sort of house party, just the three of us, and suggests the week."

He shook his head reluctantly.

"I'd like to, and I'll run up, but I can't stay a whole week. This affair of mine is most important. I have learned only today what I have been months in seeking."

And while he talked, she studied his face as only a woman in love can study a man's face. She knew every minutest detail of Winter Hall's face, from the inverted arch of the joined eyebrows to the pictured corners of the lips, from the firm uncleft chin to the last least crinkle of the ear. Being a man, even if he were in love, not so did Hall know Grunya's face. He loved her, but love did not open his eyes to microscopic details. Had he been called upon suddenly to describe her out of the registered impressions of his consciousness, he could have done so only in general terms, such as vivacious, plastic, delicate coloring, low forehead, hair always becoming, eyes that smiled and glowed even as her cheeks did, a sympathetic and adorable mouth, and a voice the viols of which were wonderful and indescribable. He had also impressions of cleanness and wholesomeness, noble seriousness, facile wit, and brilliant intellect.

What Grunya saw was a well-built man of thirty-two, with the brow of a thinker and all the facial insignia of a doer. He, too, was blue-eyed and blond, in the bronzed American way of those that live much in the sun. He smiled much, and, when he laughed, laughed heartily. Yet often, in repose, a certain sternness, almost brutal, was manifest in his face. Grunya, who loved strength and who was appalled by brutality, was sometimes troubled by fluttering divinations of this other side of his character.

Winter Hall was a rather unusual product of the times. In spite of the easy ways of wealth in which he had spent his childhood, and of the comfortable fortune inherited from his father and added to by two spinster aunts, he had early devoted himself to the cause of humanity. At college he had specialized in economics and sociology, and had been looked upon as somewhat of a crank by his less serious fellow students. Out of college, he had backed Riis, both with money and personal effort, in the New York crusade. Much time and labor spent in a social settlement had left him dissatisfied. He was always in search of the thing behind the thing, of the cause that was really the cause. Thus, he had studied politics, and, later, pursued graft from New York City to Albany and back again, and studied it, too, in the capital of his country.

After several years, apparently futile, he spent a few months in a university settlement that was in reality a hotbed of radicalism, and resolved to begin his studies from the very bottom. A year he spent as a casual laborer wandering over the country, and for another year he wandered as a vagabond, the companion of tramps and yegg men. For two years, in Chicago, he was a professional charity worker, toiling long hours and drawing down a salary of fifty dollars a month. And out of it all, he had developed into a socialist—a "millionaire socialist," as he was labeled by the press.

He traveled much, and investigated always, studying affairs at first hand. There was never a strike of importance that did not see him among the first on the ground. He attended all the national and international conventions of organized labor, and spent a year in Russia during the impending crisis of the 1905 Revolution. Many articles of his had appeared in the heavier magazines, and he was the author of several books, all well written, deep, thoughtful, and, for a socialist, conservative.

And this was the man with whom Grunya Constantine chatted and drank tea in the window-seat of her East Side apartment.

"But it is not necessary for you to keep yourself mewed up all the time in this wretched, stifling city," she was saying. "In your case I can't imagine what imperatively compels you—"

But she did not finish the sentence, for at that moment she discovered that Hall was no longer listening to her. His glance had chanced to rest on the afternoon paper lying on the seat. Entirely oblivious of her existence, he had picked up the paper and begun to read.

Grunya sulked prettily, but he took no notice of her.

"It's very nice of you, I . . . I must say," she broke out, finally attracting his attention. "Reading a newspaper while I am talking to you."

He turned the sheet so that she could see the headline of McDuffy's assassination. She looked up at him with incomprehension.

"I beg your pardon, Grunya, but when I saw that, I forgot everything." He tapped his forefinger on the headline. "That is why I am so busy. That is why I remain in New York. That is why I can allow myself no more than a week end with you, and you know how dearly I would love to have the whole week."

"But I do not understand," she faltered. "Because the anarchists have blown up a chief of police in another city . . . I . . . I don't understand."

"I'll tell you. For two years I had my suspicions, then they became a certainty, and for months now I have steadily devoted myself to running down what I believe to be the most terrible organization for assassination that has ever flourished in the United States, or anywhere else. In fact, I am almost certain that the organization is international.

"Do you remember when John Mossman committed suicide by leaping from the seventh story of the Fidelity Building? He was my friend, as well as my father's friend before me. There was no reason for him to kill himself. The Fidelity Trust Corporation was flourishing. So were all his other interests. His home life was unusually happy. His health was prodigiously good. There was nothing on his mind. Yet the stupid police called it suicide. There was some talk about its being tri-facial neuralgia—incurable, unescapable, unendurable. When men get that they do commit suicide. But he did not have it. We lunched together the day of his death. I know he did not have it, and I made a point of verifying the fact by interviewing his physician. It was theory only, and it was poppycock. He never killed himself, never leaped from the seventh story of the Fidelity Building. Then who killed him? And why? Somebody threw him from the seventh story. Who? Why?

"It is likely that the affair would have been dismissed from my mind as an insoluble mystery, had not Governor Northampton been killed by an air-rifle just three days later. You remember?—on a city street, from any one of a thousand windows. They never got a clue. I wondered casually about these two murders, and from then on, grew keenly alive to anything unusual in the daily list of homicides in the whole country.

"Oh, I shall not give you the whole list, but just a few. There was Borff, the organized labor grafter of Sannington. He had controlled that city for years. Graft prosecution after graft prosecution failed to reach him. When they settled his estate they found him possessed of half a dozen millions. They settled his estate just after he had reached out and laid hands on the whole political machinery of the state. It was just at the height of his power and his corruption when he was struck down.

"And there were others—Chief of Police Little; Welchorst, the big promoter; Blankhurst, the Cotton King; Inspector Satcherly, found floating in the East River, and so on, and so on. The perpetrators were never discovered. Then there were the society murders—Charley Atwater, killed on that last hunting trip of his; Mrs. Langthorne-Haywards; Mrs. Hastings-Reynolds; old Van Auston—oh, a long list indeed.

"All of which convinced me that a strong organization of some sort was at work. That it was no mere Black Hand affair, I was certain. The murders were not confined to any nationality nor to any stratum of society. My first thought was of the anarchists. Forgive me, Grunya—" His hand flashed out to hers and retained it warmly. "I had heard much talk of you, and that you were in close touch with the violent groups. I knew that you spent much money, and I was suspicious. And at any rate, you could put me in closer touch with the anarchists. I came suspecting you, and I remained to love you. I found you the gentlest of anarchists and a very half-hearted one at that. You were already started in your settlement work down here—"

"And you remained to dissatisfy me with that, too," she laughed, at the same time lifting the hand that held hers and resting her cheek against it. "But go on. I'm all excited."

"I did get in close with the anarchists, and the more I studied them the more confident I became that they were incapable. They were so unpractical. They dreamed dreams and spun theories and raged against police persecution, and that was all. They never got anywhere. They never did anything but get themselves in trouble—I am speaking of the violent groups, of course. As for the Tolstoians and the Kropotkinians, they were no more than mild academic philosophers. They couldn't harm a fly, and their violent cousins couldn't.

"You see, the assassinations have been of all sorts. Had they been political alone, or social, they might have been due to some hopelessly secret society. But they were commercial and society as well. Therefore, I concluded, the world must in some way have access to this organization. But how? I assumed the hypothesis that there was some man I wanted killed. And there I stuck. I did not have the address of the firm that would perform that task for me. Here was the flaw in my reasoning, namely, the hypothesis itself. I really did not want to kill any man.

"But this flaw dawned on me afterwards, when Coburn, at the Federal Club, told half a dozen of us of an adventure he had just had this afternoon. To him it was merely a curious incident, but I caught at once the gleam of light in it. He was crossing Fifth Avenue, downtown, on foot, when a man, dressed like a mechanician, dismounted alongside of him from a motorcycle and spoke to him. In a few words, the fellow told him that if there were anyone he wanted put out of the world it could be attended to with safety and dispatch. About that time Coburn threatened to punch the fellow's head, and he promptly jumped on his motorcycle and made off.

"Now here's the point. Coburn was in deep trouble. He had recently been double-crossed (if you know what that means) by Mattison, his partner, to the tune of a tremendous sum. In addition, Mattison had cleared out for Europe with Coburn's wife. Do you see? First, Coburn did have, or might be supposed to have, or ought to have, a desire for vengeance against Mattison. And secondly, thanks to the newspapers, the affair was public property."

"I see!" Grunya cried, with glowing eyes. "There was the flaw in your hypothesis. Since you could not make public your hypothetical desire to kill a man, the organization, naturally, could make no overtures to you about it."

"Correct. But I was no forwarder. Or yet, in a way, I was. I saw now how the world got access to the organization and its service. From then on I studied the mysterious and prominent murders with this in mind, and I found, so far as the society ones were concerned, that they were practically always preceded by sensational public exploitation of scandal. The commercial murders—well, the shady and unfair transactions of a fair proportion of the big businessmen are always leaking out, even though they do not get into print. When Hawthorn was found mysteriously dead on his yacht, the gossip of his underhand dealings in the fight against the Combine had been in the clubs for weeks. You may not remember them, but in their day the Atwater-Jones scandal and the Langthorne-Haywards scandal were most sensationally featured by the newspapers.

"So I became certain that this murder organization must approach persons high in political, business, and social life. And I was also certain that its overtures were not always rebuffed as in the case of Coburn. I looked about me and wondered what ones of the very men I met in the clubs or at directors' meetings had patronized this firm of men-killers. That I must be acquainted with such men I had no doubt, but which ones were they? And imagine my asking them to give me the address of the firm which they had employed to wipe out their enemies.

"But at last, and only now, have I got the direct clue. I kept close eye on all my friends who were high in the world. When any one of them was afflicted by a great trouble, I attached myself to him. For a time this was fruitless, though there was one who must have availed himself of the services of the organization, for, within six months, the man who had been the cause of his trouble was dead. Suicide, the police said.

"And then my chance came. You know of the furor of a few years ago caused by the marriage of Gladys Van Martin with Baron Portos de Moigne. It was one of those unfortunate international marriages. He was a brute. He has robbed her and divorced her. The details of his conduct have only just come out, and they are incredibly horrible. He has even beaten her so badly that the physicians despaired of her life, for a time, and, later, of her reason. And by French law he has possessed himself of their children—two boys.

"Her brother, Percy Van Martin, and I were classmates at college. I promptly made it a point to get in close with him. We've seen a good deal of each other the last several weeks. Only the other day the thing I was waiting for happened, and he told me of it. The organization had approached him. Unlike Coburn, he did not drive the man away, but heard him out. If Van Martin cared to go further in the matter, he was to insert the single word MESOPOTAMIA in the personal column of the *Herald*. I quickly persuaded him to let me take hold of the affair. I inserted MESOPOTAMIA, as directed, and, acting as Van Martin's representative, I have seen and talked with one of the men of the organization. He was only an underling, however. They are very suspicious and careful. But tonight I shall meet the principal. It is all arranged. And then . . ."

"Yes, yes," Grunya cried eagerly. "And then?"

"I don't know. I have no plans."

"But the danger!"

Hall smiled reassuringly.

"I don't imagine there will be any risk. I am coming merely to transact some business with the firm, namely, the assassination of Percy Van Martin's ex-brother-in-law. Firms do not make a practice of killing their clients."

"But when they find out you are not a client?" she protested.

"I won't be there at that time. And when they do find out, it will be too late for them to do me any harm."

"Be careful, do be careful," Grunya urged as they parted at the door half an hour later. "And you will come up for the week end?"

"Surely."

"I'll meet you at the station myself."

"And I'll meet your redoubtable uncle a few minutes afterwards, I suppose." He made a mock shiver. "He's not a regular ogre, I hope."

"You'll love him," she proclaimed proudly. "He is finer and better than a dozen fathers. He never denies me anything. Not even—"

"Me?" Hall interrupted.

Grunya tried to meet him with an equal audaciousness, but blushed and dropped her eyes, and the next moment was encircled by his arms.

4

"So you are Ivan Dragomiloff?"

Winter Hall paused a moment to glance curiously around at the book-lined walls and back again to the colorless blond in the black skullcap, who had not risen to greet him.

"I must say access to you is made sufficiently difficult. It leads one to believe that the—·er—work of your Bureau is performed discreetly as well as capably."

Dragomiloff smiled the ghost of a pleased smile.

"Sit down," he said, indicating a chair that faced him and that threw the visitor's face into the light.

Again Hall glanced around the room and back at the man before him.

"I am surprised," was Hall's comment.

"You expected low-browed ruffians and lurid melodrama, I suppose?" Dragomiloff queried pleasantly.

"No, not that. I knew too keen a mind was required to direct the operations of your—er—institution."

"They have been uniformly successful."

"How long have you been in business?—if I may ask."

"Eleven years, actively—though there was preparation and elaboration of the plan prior to that."

"You don't mind talking with me about it?" was Hall's next query.

"Certainly not," came the answer. "As a client, you are in the same boat with me. Our interests are identical. And, since we never blackmail our clients after the transaction is completed, our interests remain identical. A little important information can do no harm, and I don't mind saying that I am rather proud of this organization. It is, as you say, and if I immodestly say so myself, capably directed."

"But I can't understand," Hall exclaimed. "You are the last person in the world I should conceive of as being at the head of a band of murderers."

"And you are the last person in the world I should expect to find here seeking the professional services of such a person," was the dry counter. "I like your looks. You are strong, honest, unafraid, and in your eyes is that undefinable yet unmistakable tiredness of the scholar. You read a great deal, and study. You are as remarkably different from my regular run of clients as I am, obviously, from the person you expected to meet at the head of a band of murderers. Though executioners is the better and truer description."

"Never mind the name," Hall answered. "It does not reduce my surprise that you should be conducting this—er—enterprise."

"Ah, but you scarcely know how we conduct it." Dragomiloff laced and interlaced his strong, lean fingers and meditated for further answer. "I might explain that we conduct our trade with a greater measure of ethics than our clients bring to us."

"Ethics!" Hall burst into laughter.

"Yes, precisely; and I'll admit it sounds funny in connection with an Assassination Bureau."

"Is that what you call it?"

"One name is as good as another," the head of the Bureau went on imperturbably. "But you will find, in patronizing us, a keener, a more rigid standard of right-dealing than in the business world. I saw the need of that at the start. It was imperative. Organized as we were, outside the law, and in the very teeth of the law, success was only to be gained by doing right. We have to be right with one another, with our patrons, with everybody, and everything. You have no idea the amount of business we turn away."

"What!" Hall cried. "And why?"

"Because it would not be right to transact it. Don't laugh, please. In fact, we of the Bureau are all rather fanatical when it comes to ethics. We have the sanction of right in all that we do. We must have that sanction. Without it we could not last very long. Believe me, this is so. And now to business. You have come here through the accredited channels. You can have but one errand. Whom do you want executed?"

"You don't know?" Hall asked in wonderment.

"Certainly not. That is not my branch. I spend no time drumming up trade."

"Perhaps, when I give you the man's name, you will not find that sanction of right. It seems you are judge as well as executioner."

"Not executioner. I never execute. It is not my branch. I am the head. I judge—locally, that is—and other members carry out the orders."

"But suppose these others should prove weak vessels?"

Dragomiloff looked very pleased.

"Ah, that was the rub. I studied it a long time. Almost as conclusively as anything else, it was that very thing that made me see that our operations could be conducted only on an ethical basis. We have our own code of right, and our own law. Only men of the highest ethical nature, combined with the requisite physical and nervous stamina, are admitted to our ranks. As a result, almost fanatically are our oaths observed. There have been weak vessels—several of them." He paused and seemed to ponder sadly. "They paid the penalty. It was a splendid object lesson to the rest."

"You mean—?"

"Yes; they were executed. It had to be. But it is very rarely necessary with us."

"How do you manage it?"

"When we have selected a desperate, intelligent, and reasonable man—this selecting, by the way, is done by the members themselves, who, rubbing shoulders everywhere with all sorts of men, have better opportunity than I for meeting and estimating strong characters. When such a man is selected, he is tried out. His life is the pledge he gives for his faithfulness and loyalty. I know of these men, and have the reports on them. I rarely see them, unless they rise in the organization, and by the same token very few of them ever see me.

"One of the first things done is to give a candidate an unimportant and unremunerative murder—say, a brutal mate of some ship, or a bullying foreman, a usurer, or a petty grafting politician. It is good for the world to have such individuals out of it, you know. But to return. Every step of the candidate in this, his first killing, is so marked by us that a mass of testimony is gathered sufficient to convict him before any court in this land. And the affair is so conducted that this testimony proceeds from outside persons. We would not have to appear. For that matter, we have never found it necessary to invoke the country's law for the castigation of a member.

"Well, when this initial task has been performed, the man is one of us, tied to us body and soul. After that he is thoroughly educated in our methods—"

"Does ethics enter into the curriculum?" Hall interrupted to ask.

"It does, it does," was the enthusiastic response. "It is the most important thing we teach our members. Nothing that is not founded on right can endure."

"You are an anarchist?" the visitor asked with sharp irrelevance.

The Chief of the Assassination Bureau shook his head.

"No; I am a philosopher."

"It is the same thing."

"With a difference. For instance, the anarchists mean well; but I do well. Of what use is philosophy that cannot be applied? Take the old-country anarchists. They decide on an assassination. They plan and conspire night and day, at last strike the blow, and are almost invariably captured by the police. Usually the person or personage they try to kill gets off unscathed. Not so with us."

"Don't you ever fail?"

"We strive to make failure impossible. Any member who fails, because of weakness or fear, is punished with death." Dragomiloff paused solemnly, his pale blue eyes shining with an exultant light. "We have never had a failure. Or course, we give a man a year in which to perform his task. Also, if it be a big affair, he is given assistants. And I repeat, we have never had a failure. The organization is as near perfect as the mind of man can make it. Even if I should drop out of it, die suddenly, the organization would run on just the same."

"Do you draw any line at accepting commissions?" Winter Hall asked.

"No; from emperor and king down to the humblest peasant —we accept them all, if—and it is a big *if*—if their execution is decided to be socially justifiable. And, once we have accepted payment, which is in advance, you know, and have decided it to be right to make a certain killing, that killing takes place. It is one of our rules."

As Winter Hall listened, a wild idea flashed into his mind. So whimsical was it, so almost lunatic, that he felt immeasurably fascinated by it.

"You are very ethical, I must say," he began, "a—what I might call—ethical enthusiast."

"Or monstrosity," Dragomiloff added pleasantly. "Yes, I have quite a penchant that way."

"Anything you conceive to be right, that thing you will do."

Dragomiloff nodded affirmation, and a silence fell, which he was the first to break.

"You have some one in mind whom you wish removed. Who is it?"

"I am so curious," was the reply, "and so interested, that I should like to approach it tentatively . . . you know, in arranging the terms of the bargain. You surely must have a scale of prices, determined, of course, by the position and influence of . . . of the victim."

Dragomiloff nodded.

"Suppose it were a king I wished removed?" Hall queried.

"There are kings and kings. The price varies. Is your man a king?"

"No; he is not a king. He is a strong man, but not of noble title."

"He is not a president?" Dragomiloff asked quickly.

"No; he holds no official position whatever. In fact, he is a man in private life. For what sum will you guarantee the removal of a man in private life?"

"For such a man it would be less difficult and hazardous. He would come cheaper."

"Not so," Hall urged. "I can afford to be generous in this. It is a very difficult and hazardous commission I am giving you. He is a man of powerful mind, of infinite wit and recourse."

"A millionaire?"

"I do not know."

"I would suggest forty thousand dollars as the price," the head of the Bureau concluded. "Of course, on learning his identity, I may have to increase that sum. On the other hand, I may decrease it."

Hall drew bills of large denomination from his pocketbook, counted them, and handed them to the other.

"I imagined you did business on a currency basis," he said, "and so I came prepared. And, now, as I understand it, you will guarantee to kill—"

"I do no killing," Dragomiloff interrupted.

"You will guarantee to have killed any man I name."

"That is correct, with the proviso, of course, that an investigation shows his execution to be justifiable."

"Good. I understand perfectly. Any man I name, even if he should be my father, or yours?"

"Yes; though as it happens I have neither father nor son."

"Suppose I named myself?"

"It would be done. The order would go forth. We have no concern with the whims of our clients."

"But suppose, say tomorrow or next week, I should change my mind?"

"It would be too late." Dragomiloff spoke with decision. "Once an order goes forth it can never be recalled. That is one of the most necessary of our rules."

"Very good. However, I am not the man."

"Then who is he?"

"The name men know him by is Ivan Dragomiloff."

Hall said it quietly enough, and just as quietly was it received.

"I want better identification," Dragomiloff suggested.

"He is a native of Russia, I believe. I know he is a resident of New York City. He is blond, remarkably blond, and of just about your size, height, weight, and age."

Dragomiloff's pale-blue eyes looked long and steadily at his visitor. At last he spoke.

"I was born in the province of Valenko. Where was your man born?"

"In the province of Valenko."

Again Dragomiloff scrutinized the other with unwavering eyes.

"I am compelled to believe that you mean me."

Hall nodded unequivocally.

"It is, believe me, unprecedented," Dragomiloff went on. "I am puzzled. Frankly, I cannot understand why you want my life. I have never seen you before. We do not know each other. I cannot guess at the remotest motive. At any rate, you forget that I must have a sanction of right before I order this execution."

"I am prepared to furnish it," was Hall's answer.

"But you must convince me."

"I am prepared to do that. It was because I divined you to be what you called yourself, an ethical monstrosity, that I conceived this proposition and made it to you. I believe, if I can prove to you the justification of your death, that you will carry it out. Am I right?"

"You are right." Dragomiloff paused, and then his face lighted up with a smile. "Of course, that would be suicide, and you know that this is an Assassination Bureau."

"You would give the order to one of your members. As I understand, under pledge of his own life he would be compelled to carry out the order."

Dragomiloff looked even pleased.

"Very true. It goes to show how perfect is the machine I have created. It is fitted to every contingency, even to this most unexpected one developed by you. Come. You interest me. You are original. You have imagination, fantasy. Pray show me the ethical sanction for my own removal from this world."

"Thou shalt not kill," Hall began.

"Pardon me," came the interruption. "We must get a basis for this discussion, which I fear will quickly become academic. The point is, you must prove to me that I have done such wrong that my death is right. And I am to be judge. What wrong have I done? What person, not a wrong-doer, have I ordered executed? In what way have I violated my own sanctions of right conduct, or even have done wrong blunderingly or unwittingly?"

"I understand, and I change my discourse accordingly. First, let me ask if you were responsible for the death of John Mossman?"

Dragomiloff nodded.

"He was a friend of mine. I had known him all my life. There was no evil in him. He harmed no one."

Hall was speaking warmly, but the other's raised hand and amused smile made him pause.

"It was something like seven years ago that John Mossman built the Fidelity Building. Where did he get the money? It was at that time that he, who had all his life been a banker in a small, conservative way, suddenly branched out in a number of large enterprises. You remember the fortune he left. Where did he get it?"

Hall was about to speak, but Dragomiloff signified that he had not finished.

"Not long before the building of the Fidelity, you will remember, the Combine attacked Carolina Steel, bankrupted it, and then absorbed the wreckage for a song. The president of Carolina Steel committed suicide—"

"To escape the penitentiary," Hall interpolated.

"He was tricked into doing what he did."

Hall nodded and said, "I recollect. It was one of the agents of the Combine."

"That agent was John Mossman."

Hall remained incredulously silent, while the other continued.

"I assure you I can prove it, and I will. But do me the courtesy of accepting for a moment whatever statements I make. They will be proved, and to your satisfaction."

"Very well then. You killed Stolypin."

"No; not guilty. The Russian Terrorists did that."

"I have your word?"

"You have my word."

Hall ranged over in his mind all the assassinations he had tabulated, and made another departure.

"James and Hardman, president and secretary of the Southwestern Federation of Miners—"

"We killed them," Dragomiloff broke in. "And what was wrong about it—mind you, wrong to me?"

"You are a humanist. The cause of labor, as that of the people, must be dear to you. It was a great loss to organized labor, the deaths of these two leaders."

"On the contrary," Dragomiloff replied. "They were killed in 1904. For six years prior to that, the Federation had won not one victory, while it had been decisively beaten in three disastrous strikes. In the first six months after the two leaders were removed, the Federation won the big strike of 1905, and from then to now has never ceased making substantial gains."

"You mean?" Hall demanded.

"I mean that the Mine Owners League did not bring about the assassination. I mean that James and Hardman were secretly in the pay, and in big pay, of the Mine Owners League. I mean that it was a group of the miners themselves that laid the facts of their leaders' treason before us and paid the price we demanded for the service. We did it for twenty-five thousand dollars."

Winter Hall's bafflement plainly showed, and he debated a long minute before speaking.

"I believe you, Mr. Dragomiloff. Tomorrow or next day I should like to go over the proofs with you. But that will be merely for formal correctness. In the meantime I must find some other way to convince you. This list of assassinations is a long one."

"Longer than you think."

"And I do not doubt but what you have found similar justification for all of them. Mind you, not that I believe any one of these killings to be right, but that I believe they have been right to you. Your fear that the discussion would become academic was well founded. It is only in that way that I can hope to get you. Suppose we defer it until tomorrow. Will you lunch with me? Or where would you prefer us to meet?"

"Right here, I think, after lunch." Dragomiloff waved his hand around at his book-covered walls. "There are plenty of authorities, you see, and we can always send out to the branch Carnegie Library around the corner for more."

He pressed the call button, and both arose as the servant entered.

"Believe me, I am going to get you," was Hall's parting assurance.

Dragomiloff smiled whimsically.

"I trust not," he said. "But if you do it will be unique."

5

For long days and nights the discussion between Hall and Dragomiloff was waged. At first confined to ethics, it quickly grew wider and deeper. Ethics being the capstone of all the sciences, they found themselves compelled to seek down through those sciences to the original foundations. Dragomiloff demanded of Hall's *Thou shalt not kill* a more rigid philosophic sanction than religion had given it. While, in order to be intelligible, and to reason intelligently, they found it necessary to thresh out and ascertain each other's most ultimate beliefs and telic ideals.

It was the struggle of two scholars, and practical scholars at that; yet more often than not the final result sought was lost in the excitement and clash of ideas. And Hall did his antagonist the justice of realizing that on his part it was purely a pursuit of truth. That his life was the forfeit if he lost had no influence on Dragomiloff's reasoning. The question at issue was whether or not his Assassination Bureau was a right institution.

Hall's one thesis, which he never abandoned, to which he forced all roads of argument to lead, was that the time had come in the evolution of society when society, as a whole, must work out its own salvation. The time was past, he contended, for the man on horseback, or for small groups of men on horseback, to manage the destinies of society. Dragomiloff, he insisted, was such a man, and his Assassination Bureau was the steed he bestrode, by virtue of which he judged and punished, and, within narrow limits it was true, herded and trampled society in the direction he wanted it to go.

Dragomiloff, on the other hand, did not deny that he played

the part of the man on horseback, who thought for society, decided for society, and drove society; but he did deny, and emphatically, that society as a whole was able to manage itself, and that, despite blunders and mistakes, social progress lay in such management of the whole by itself. And this was the crux of the question, to settle which they ransacked history and traced the social evolution of man up from the minutest known details of primitive groupings to highest civilization.

In fact, so practical-minded were the two scholars, so unmetaphysical, that they accepted social expediency as the determining factor and agreed that it was in the highest way ethical. And in the end, measured by this particular yardstick, Winter Hall won. Dragomiloff acknowledged his own defeat, and, in his gratification and excitement, Hall's hand went impulsively out to him. Firmly, and despite his surprise, Dragomiloff returned the grip.

"I see, now," he said, "that I failed to lay sufficient stress on the social factors. The assassinations have not been so much intrinsically wrong as socially wrong. I even take part of that back. As between individuals, they have not been wrong at all. But individuals are not individuals alone. They are parts of complexes of individuals. There was where I erred. It is dimly clear to me. I was not justified. And now—" He broke off and looked at his watch. "It is two o'clock. We have sat late. And now I am prepared to pay the penalty. Of course you will give me time to settle my affairs before I give the order to my agents?"

Hall, who in the height of debate had forgotten the terms of the debate, was startled.

"I am not prepared for that," he said. "And to tell the truth, it had quite slipped my mind. Perhaps it is not necessary. You are yourself convinced of the wrong of assassination. Suppose you disband the organization. That will be sufficient."

But Dragomiloff shook his head.

"An agreement is an agreement. I have accepted a commission from you. Right is right, and this is where, I maintain, the doctrine of social expediency does not apply. The individual, per se, has some prerogatives left, and one of these is the keeping of one's word. This I must do. The commission shall be carried out. I am afraid it will be the last handled by the Bureau. This is Saturday morning. Suppose you give me until tomorrow night before issuing the order?"

"Tommyrot!" Hall exclaimed.

"That is not argument," was the grave reproof. "Besides, all argument is finished. I decline to hear any more. One thing, though, in fairness: considering how difficult a person I shall be to assassinate, I would suggest a further charge of at least ten thousand dollars." He held up his hand in token that he had more to say. "Oh, believe me, I am modest. I shall make it so difficult for my agents that it will be worth all of fifty thousand and more——"

"If you will only break up the organization——"

But Dragomiloff silenced him.

"The discussion is ended. This is now my affair. The organization will be broken up in any event, but I warn you, according to our rules of long standing, I may escape. As you will recollect, I promised you, at the time the bargain was made, that if, at the end of a year, the commission had not been fulfilled, the fee would be returned to you plus five percent. If I escape I shall hand it to you myself."

But Winter Hall waved his hand impatiently.

"Listen," he said. "I insist on one statement. You and I are agreed on the foundation of ethics. Social expedience being the basis of all ethics——"

"Pardon me——" came the interruption "——of social ethics only. The individual, in certain aspects, is still an individual."

"Neither you nor I," Hall continued, "accepts the old Judaic code of an eye for an eye. We do not believe in punishment for crime. The killings of your Bureau, while justified by crimes committed by the victims, were not regarded by you as punishments. You looked upon your victims as social ills, the extirpation of which would benefit society. You removed them from the social organism on the same principle that surgeons remove cancers. I caught that point of view of yours from the beginning of the discussion.

"But to return. Not accepting the punishment theory, you and I regard crime as a mere anti-social tendency, and as such, expediently and arbitrarily, we classify it. Thus, crime is a social abnormality, partaking of the nature of sickness. It *is* sickness. The criminal, the wrong-doer, is a sick man, and he should be treated accordingly, so that he may be cured of his sickness.

"Now I come to you and to my point. Your Assassination Bureau was anti-social. You believed in it. Therefore you were sick. Your belief in assassination constituted your sickness. But now you no longer believe. You are cured. Your tendency is no longer anti-social. There is now no need for your death, which would be nothing else than punishment for an illness of which you had already been cured. Disband the organization and go out of business. That is all you have to do."

"Are you done—quite done?" Dragomiloff queried suavely.

"Yes."

"Then let me answer and end the argument. I conceived my Bureau in righteousness, and I operated it in righteousness. Also, I created it, made it the perfect thing that it is. Its foundation was certain right principles. In all its history, not one of these principles was violated. A particular one of these principles was that portion of the contracts with our clients wherein we guaranteed to carry out any commission we accepted. I accepted a commission from you. I received forty thousand dollars. The agreement was that I should order my own execution if you proved to my satisfaction that the assassinations achieved by the Bureau were wrong. You have proved it. Nothing remains but to live up to the agreement.

"I am proud of this institution. Nor shall I, with a last act, stultify its basic principles, break the rules under which it operated. This I hold is my right as an individual, and in no way does it conflict with social expediency. I do not want to die. If I escape death for a year, the commission I accepted from you, as you know, automatically terminates. I shall do my best to escape. And now, not another word. I am resolved. Concerning breaking up the Bureau, what would you suggest?"

"Give me the names and all details of all members. I shall then serve notice on them to disband—"

"Not until after my death or until the year has expired," Dragomiloff objected.

"All right, after your death, or the expiration of the year, I shall serve this notice, backed by the threat of going to the police with my information."

"They may kill you," was the warning.

"Yes; they may. I shall have to take that chance."

"You can avoid it. When you serve notice, inform them that all information is placed in escrow in half a dozen different cities, and that in event of your being killed it goes into the hands of the police."

It was three in the morning before the details for disbanding the organization were arranged. It was at this time that a long silence fell, broken at last by Dragomiloff.

"Do you know, Hall, I like you. You are an ethical enthusiast yourself. You might almost have created the Bureau, than which I know no higher compliment, because it is my belief that the Bureau is a remarkable achievement. At any rate, not only do I like you, but I know I can trust you. You would keep your word as I keep mine. Now, I have a daughter. Her mother is dead and in the event of my death she would be without kith or kin in the world. I should like to put her in your charge. Are you willing to accept the responsibility?"

Hall nodded his acquiescence.

"She is a grown woman, so there is no need for guardianship papers. But she is unmarried, and I shall leave her a great deal of money, the investment of which you will have to see to. I am running out to see her this afternoon. Will you come along? It is not far, only at Edge Moor on the Hudson."

"Why, I'm making a week-end visit to Edge Moor myself!" Hall exclaimed.

"Good. Whereabouts in Edge Moor?"

"I don't know. I've never been there."

"Never mind. It is not a large place. You can spare a couple of hours Sunday morning. I'll run over for you in a machine. Telephone me where and when to come. Suburban 245 is my number."

Hall jotted the number down and rose to go.

Dragomiloff yawned as they shook hands.

"I wish you would reconsider," the other urged.

But Dragomiloff yawned again, shook his head, and showed his visitor out.

6

Grunya ran the machine that carried Winter Hall from the station at Edge Moor.

"Uncle is really eager to meet you," she assured him. "He doesn't know who you are, yet. I teased him by not telling him. Perhaps it is the teasing that accounts for his eagerness, for he certainly is eager."

"Have you told him?" Hall asked significantly.

Grunya became suddenly absorbed in operating the car.

"What?" she asked.

For reply, Hall laid his hand on hers upon the steering wheel. She ventured one glance at him, looking into his eyes with audacious steadiness for a moment. Then the telltale flush betrayed her, the steady gaze wavered, and with dropped eyes she returned to the steering.

"That might account for his eagerness," Hall remarked quietly.

"I—I never thought of it."

Her eyes were turned from him, but he could see the rosy warmth in her cheek. After a minute he made another remark.

"It is a pity to shame so splendid a sunset with unveraciousness."

"Coward," she cried; but her enunciation made the epithet a love note.

And then she looked at him again, and laughed, and he laughed with her, and both felt that the sunset was unsmirched and that the world was very fair.

It was when they entered the driveway to the bungalow that he asked her in what direction lay the Dragomiloff place.

"Never heard of it," was her response. "Dragomiloff? No such person lives in Edge Moor, I am sure. Why?"

"They may be recent comers," he suggested.

"Perhaps so. And here we are. Grosset, take Mr. Hall's suitcase. Where's Uncle?"

"In the library, writing, miss. He said not to disturb him till dinner."

"Then at dinner you'll meet," she said to Hall. "And you'll only just have time. Show Mr. Hall his room, Grosset."

Fifteen minutes later, Winter Hall, in the absence of Grunya, entered the living room and found himself face to face with the man he had parted from at three that morning.

"What the devil are you doing here?" Hall blurted out.

But the other's composure was unshaken.

"Waiting to be introduced, I suppose," he said, holding out his hand. "I am Sergius Constantine. Grunya has certainly surprised both of us."

"And you are also Ivan Dragomiloff?"

"Yes; but not in this house."

"But I do not understand. You spoke of a daughter."

"Grunya is my daughter, though she believes herself my niece. It is a long story, which I shall make short, after dinner, when we get rid of Grunya. But let me tell you now, that the situation is beautiful, gratifyingly beautiful. You, whom I selected to watch over my Grunya, I find are already—if I am right—her lover. Am I right?"

"I—I don't know what to say," Hall faltered, his wit for one time not ready, his mind stunned by this most undreamed dénouement.

"Am I right?" Dragomiloff repeated.

"You are right," came the answer, prompt at last. "I do love—her—I do love Grunya. But does she know . . . you?"

"Only as her uncle, Sergius Constantine, head of the importing house of that name—here she comes. As I was saying, I agree with you in preferring Turgenev to Tolstoy. Of course, this without detracting from the power of Tolstoy. It is Tolstoy's philosophy that is repugnant to one who believes—ah, here you are, Grunya."

"And already acquainted," she pouted. "I had expected to be present at such a momentous encounter." She turned chidingly to Hall, while Constantine's arm encircled her waist. "Why didn't you warn me you could dress with such speed?"

She held out her free hand to him.

"Come," she said, "let us go in to dinner."

And in this manner, Constantine's arm around Grunya, and she lightly leading Hall by the hand, the three passed into the dining room.

At table Hall caught himself desiring to pinch himself in order to disprove the reality of which he was a part. The situation was almost too preposterously grotesque to be real—Grunya, whom he loved, alternately tilting and smiling at her father whom she believed her uncle, and whom she never dreamed was the originator and head of the dread Assassination Bureau; he, Hall, whom Grunya loved in return, joining in the badinage against the man to whom he had paid fifty thousand dollars to order his own execution; and Dragomiloff himself, unperturbed, complacent, unbending in the general mirth, until his habitual frostiness thawed into actual geniality.

Afterwards, Grunya played and sang, until Dragomiloff, under the double plea of an expected visitor and a desire for a man-talk with Hall, advised her, in mock phrases of paternal patronage, that it was bedtime for a chit of her years. With a parting fling, she said good night and left them, her laughter rippling back through the open door. Dragomiloff got up, closed it, and returned to his seat.

"Well?" Hall demanded.

"My father was a contractor in the Russian-Turkish War," was the reply. "His name was—well, never mind his name. He made a fortune of sixty million rubles, which I, as an only son, inherited. At university I became inoculated with radical ideas and joined the Young Russians. We were a pack of Utopianists and dreamers, and of course we got into trouble. I was in prison several times. My wife died of smallpox at the same time that her brother Sergius Constantine died of the same disease. This took place on my last estate. Our latest conspiracy had leaked, and this time it meant Siberia for me. My escape was simple. My brother-in-law, a pronounced conservative, was buried under my name, and I became Sergius Constantine. Grunya was a baby. I got out of the country easily enough, though what was left of my fortune fell into the hands of the officials. Here in New York, where Russian spies are more prevalent than you imagine, I maintained the fiction of my name. And there you have it. I have even returned once to Russia, as my brother-in-law, of course, and sold out his possessions. Too long did I maintain the fiction; Grunya knew me as her uncle, and her uncle I have remained. That is all."

"But the Assassination Bureau?" Hall asked.

"Believing it was right, and stung by the charge that we Russians were thinkers, not doers, I organized it. And it has worked, successfully, perfectly. It has been a financial success as well. I proved that I could act, as well as dream dreams. Grunya, however, still calls me a dreamer. But she does not know. One moment."

He went into the adjoining room and returned with a large envelope in his hand.

"And now to other things. My expected visitor is the man to whom I shall give the order of execution. I intended to do so tomorrow, but your opportune presence tonight expedites matters. Here are my instructions to you." He handed over the envelope. "Grunya, legally, must sign all papers, deeds, and such things, but you must advise her. My will is in my safe. You will have to handle my funds for me until I die or return. If I telegraph for money, or anything, you will do as instructed. In this envelope is the cipher I shall use, which is likewise the cipher used by the organization.

"There is a large emergency fund which I have handled for the Bureau. This belongs to the members. I shall make you its custodian. The members will draw upon it at need." Dragomiloff shook his head with simulated sadness and smiled. "I am afraid I shall prove very expensive to them before they get me."

"Heavens, man!" Hall cried. "You are furnishing them the sinews of war. What you should do is to prevent their access to the fund."

"That would not be fair, Hall. And I am so made that I must play fairly. And I do you the honor to believe that in the matter you will likewise play fairly and obey all my instructions. Am I right?"

"But you are asking me to furnish aid to the men who are going to kill you, the father of the girl I love. It is preposterous. It is monstrous. Put a stop to the whole thing now. Disband the organization and be done with it."

But Dragomiloff was adamant.

"My mind is made up. You know that. I must do what I believe to be right. You will obey my instructions?"

"You are a monster! A stubborn, stiff-necked monster of absurd and lunatic righteousness. You are a scholar's mind degraded, you are ethics gone mad, you are . . . are . . ."

But Winter Hall failed in his quest for further superlatives, and stuttered, and ceased. Dragomiloff smiled patiently.

"You will obey my instructions. Am I right?"

"Yes, yes, yes. I'll obey them," Hall cried angrily. "It is patent that you will have your way. There is no stopping you. But why tonight? Won't tomorrow be time enough to start on this madman's adventure?"

"No; I am eager to start. And you have hit the precise word. Adventure. That is it. I have not had it since I was a boy, since I was a young Bakuninite in Russia dreaming my boyish dreams of universal human freedom. Since then, what have I done? I have been a thinking machine. I have built up successful businesses. I have made a fortune. I have invented the Assassination

Bureau and run it. And that is all. I have not lived. I have had no adventure. I have been a mere spider, a huge brain thinking and planning in the midst of a web. But now I break the web. I go forth on the adventure path. Why, do you know, I have never killed a man in my life. Nor have I ever seen one killed. I was never in a railroad accident. I know nothing of violence; I who possess the vast strength of violence have never used that strength save in amity, in boxing and wrestling and such exercises. Now I shall live, body and brain, and play a new role. Strength!"

He held out his lean white hand and looked at it angrily.

"Grunya will tell you that I can bend a silver dollar between those fingers. Was that all they were made for?—to bend dollars? Here, your arm a moment."

Merely between fingertips and thumb, he caught Hall's forearm midway from wrist to elbow. He pressed, and Hall was startled by the fierce pang of the bruise. It seemed as if fingers and thumb would meet through the flesh and bone. The next moment the arm was flung aside, and Dragomiloff was smiling grimly.

"No damage," he said, "though it will be black and blue for a week or so. Now do you know why I want to get out of my web? I have vegetated for a score of years. I have used those fingers to write my signature and to turn the pages of books. From my web I have sent men out on the adventure path. Now I shall play against those men, and I, too, shall do. It will be a royal game. Mine was the master mind that made the perfect machine. I created it. Never has it failed to destroy the man appointed. I am now the man appointed. The question is: *is it greater than I, its creator?* Will it destroy its creator, or will its creator outwit it?"

He stopped abruptly, looked at his watch, and pressed a bell.

"Have the car brought around," he told the servant who responded, "put into it the suitcase you will find in my bedroom."

He turned to Hall as the servant left the room.

"And now my hegira begins. Haas should be here any moment."

"Who is Haas?"

"Bar none and absolutely the most capable member we have. He has always been given our most difficult and hazardous commissions. He is an ethical fanatic, a Danite. No destroying angel was ever so terrible as he. He is a flame. He is not a man at all, but a flame. You shall see for yourself. There he is now."

A moment later the man was shown in. Hall was shocked by the first view of his face—a wasted, ravaged face, hollow-cheeked and sunken, in which burned a pair of eyes the like of which could be experienced only in nightmares. Such was the fire of them that the whole face seemed caught up in the conflagration.

Hall acknowledged the introduction, and was surprised at the firm, almost savagely firm, grip of the handshake. He noted the man's movements as he took a chair and seated himself. He seemed to move cat-like, and Hall was confident that he was muscled like a tiger, though all this was belied by the withered, blighted face, which gave an impression that the rest of the body was a shrunken slender shell. Slender the body was, but Hall could mark the bulge of the biceps and shoulder muscles.

"I have a commission for you, Mr. Haas," Dragomiloff began. "Possibly it may prove the most dangerous and difficult one you have ever undertaken."

Hall could have sworn that the man's eyes blazed even more fiercely at the intimation.

"This case has received my sanction," Dragomiloff continued. "It is right, essentially right. The man must die. The Bureau has received fifty thousand dollars for his death. According to our custom, one-third of this sum will go to you. But so difficult am I afraid it will prove, that I have decided your share shall be one-half. Here are five thousand for expenses—"

"The amount is unusual," Haas broke in, licking his lips as if they were parched by the flame of his being.

"The man you are to kill is unusual," Dragomiloff retorted. "You will need to call upon Schwartz and Harrison immediately to assist you. If, after a time, the three of you have failed—"

Haas snorted incredulously, and the fever that seemed consuming him burned up with increasing heat in his lean and avid face.

"If, after a time, the three of you have failed, call upon the whole organization."

"Who is the man?" Haas demanded, and he bit the words out almost in a snarl.

"One moment." Dragomiloff turned to Hall. "What shall you tell Grunya?"

Hall considered for a space.

"A half-truth will do. I sketched the organization to her before I knew you. I can tell her you are menaced. That will suffice. And no matter what the outcome, she need never know the rest."

Dragomiloff bowed his approbation.

"Mr. Hall is to serve as secretary," he explained to Haas. "He has the cipher. All applications for money and everything else will be made to him. Keep him informed from time to time of progress."

"Who is the man?" Haas rasped out again.

"One minute, Mr. Haas. There is one thing I want to impress on you. Your pledge you remember. No matter who the person may be, you know that you must perform the task. You know in every way you must avoid risking your own life. You know what failure means, that all your comrades are sworn to kill you if you fail."

"I know all that," Haas interrupted. "It is unnecessary."

"It is my wish to have you absolutely straight on this point. No matter who the person—"

"Father, brother, wife—ay, the devil himself, or God—I understand. Who is the man? Where will I find him? You know me. When I have anything to do, I want to do it."

Dragomiloff turned to Hall with a smile of gratification.

"As I told you, I selected our best agent."

"We are wasting time," Haas muttered impatiently.

"Very well," Dragomiloff answered. "Are you ready?"

"Yes."

"Now?"

"Now."

"I, Ivan Dragomiloff, am the man."

Haas was staggered by the unexpectedness of it.

"You?" he whispered, as if louder speech had been scorched from his throat.

"I," Dragomiloff answered simply.

"Then there is no time like now," Hass said swiftly, at the same time moving his right hand towards his side pocket.

But even more swift was the leap of Dragomiloff upon him. Before Hall could rise from his chair the thing had happened and the danger was past. He saw Dragomiloff's two thumbs, end on, crooked and rigid, drive into the two hollows at either side of the base of Haas's neck. So quickly that it was practically simultaneous, at the instant of the first driven contact of the thumbs, Haas's hand stopped moving in the direction of the weapon in his pocket. Both his hands shot up and clutched spasmodically at the other's hands. Haas's face was distorted in an expression of incredible and absolute agony. He writhed and twisted for a minute, then his eyes closed, his hands dropped, his body went limp, and Dragomiloff eased him down to the floor, the flame of him quenched in unconsciousness.

Dragomiloff rolled him on his face, and, with a handkerchief, knotted his hands behind his back. He worked quickly, and as he worked he talked.

"Observe, Hall, the first anaesthetic ever used in surgery. It is purely mechanical. The thumbs press on the carotid arteries, shutting off the blood supply to the brain. The Japanese practiced it in surgical operations for centuries. If I had held the pressure for a minute or so more, the man would be dead. As it is, he will regain consciousness in a few seconds. See! He is moving now."

He rolled Haas over on his back; his eyes fluttered open and rested on Dragomiloff's face in a puzzled way.

"I told you it was a difficult case, Mr. Haas," Dragomiloff assured him. "You have failed in the first attempt. I am afraid that you will fail many times."

"You'll give a run for my money, I guess," was the answer. "Though why you want to be killed is beyond me."

"But I don't want to be killed."

"Then why under the sun have you given me the order?"

"That's my business, Mr. Haas. And it is your business to see that you do your best. How does your throat feel?"

The recumbent man rolled his head back and forth.

"Sore," he announced.

"It is a trick you ought to learn."

"I know it now," Haas rejoined, "and I am very much aware of the precise place in which to insert the thumbs. What are you going to do with me?"

"Take you along with me in the car and drop you by the roadside. It's a warm night, so you won't catch cold. If I left you here, Mr. Hall might untie you before I got started. And now I think I'll bother you for that weapon in your coat-pocket."

Dragomiloff leaned over, and from the pocket in question drew forth an automatic pistol.

"Loaded for big game and cocked and ready," he said, examining it. "All he had to do was to drop the safety lever with his thumb and pull the trigger. Will you walk to the car with me, Mr. Haas?"

Haas shook his head.

"This is more comfortable than the roadside."

For reply, Dragomiloff bent over him and lightly effected his terrible thumb grip on the throat.

"I'll walk," Haas gasped.

Quickly and lightly, though his arms were tied behind him,

and apparently without effort, the recumbent man rose to his feet, giving Hall a hint of the tiger-muscles with which he was endowed.

"It's all right," Haas grumbled. "I'm not kicking, and I'll take my medicine. But you caught me unexpectedly, and I'll tell you one thing. It is that you can't do it again, or anything else."

Dragomiloff turned and spoke to Hall.

"The Japanese claim seven different death-touches, but I only know four. And this man dreams he could best me in physical encounter. Mr. Haas, let me tell you one thing. You see the edge of my hand. Omitting the death-touches and everything else, merely using the edge of that hand like a cleaver, I can break your bones, disjoint your joints, and rupture your tendons. Pretty good, eh, for the thinking machine you have always known? Come on; let us start. This way for the adventure path. Goodbye, Hall."

The front door closed behind them, and Winter Hall, stupefied, looked about him at the modern room in which he stood. He was more pervaded than ever by the impression of unrealness. Yet that was a grand piano over there, and those were the current magazines on the reading table. He even glanced over their familiar names in an effort to orient himself. He wondered if he were going to wake up in a few minutes. He glanced at the titles of a table-rack of books—evidently Dragomiloff's. There, incongruously cheek by jowl, were Mahan's *Problem of Asia*, Buckner's *Force and Matter*, Wells's *Mr. Polly*, Nietzsche's *Beyond Good and Evil*, Jacobs's *Many Cargoes*, Veblen's *Theory of the Leisure Class*, Hyde's *From Epicurus to Christ*, and Henry James's latest novel—all forsaken by this strange mind which had closed the page of its life on books and fared forth into an impossible madness of adventure.

7

"There is no use waiting for your uncle," Hall told Grunya next morning. "We must eat breakfast and start for town."

"We?" she asked in frank wonder. "What for?"

"To get married. Before his departure, your uncle made me your unofficial guardian, and it seems to me that the best thing to do is to make my position official—that is, if you have no serious objections."

"I have, decidedly," was her reply. "In the first place, I dislike being bullied into anything, even into so gratifying a thing as marriage with you. And next, I detest mystery. Where is Uncle? What has happened? Where did he go? Did he catch an early train for the city? And why should he go to the city on Sunday?"

Hall looked at her gloomily.

"Grunya, I am not going to tell you to be brave and all that fol-de-rol. I know you, and it is unnecessary." He noted growing alarm in her face and hurried on. "I don't know when your uncle will return. I don't know if he will ever return, or if you will ever see him again. Listen. You remember that Assassination Bureau I told you about?"

She nodded.

"Well, it has selected him for its next victim. He has fled, that is all, in an attempt to escape."

"Oh! But this is outrageous!" she cried. "My Uncle Sergius! This is the twentieth century. They don't do things like that now. This is some joke you and he are playing on me."

And Hall, wondering what she would think if she knew the whole truth concerning her uncle, smiled grimly.

"On my honor, it is true," he assured her. "Your uncle has been selected as the next victim. You remember he was writing a great deal yesterday afternoon. He had had his warning and was getting his affairs in shape and preparing his instructions for me."

"But the police. Why has he not appealed to them for protection from this band of cutthroats?"

"Your uncle is a peculiar man. He won't listen to any suggestion of the police. Furthermore, he has made me promise to keep the police out of it."

"But not me," she interrupted, starting towards the door. "I shall call them up at once."

Hall caught her by the wrist, and she swung angrily around on him.

"Listen, dear," he said placatingly. "The whole thing is madness, I know. It is the sheerest impossible lunacy. Yet it is so, it is true, every last bit of it. Your uncle does not want the police brought in. It is his wish. It is his command to me. If you violate his wish, it will be because I have made the mistake of telling you. I am confident I have made no mistake."

He released her, and she hesitated on the threshold.

"It can't be!" she exclaimed. "It is unbelievable! It—it—oh, you are joking!"

"It is unbelievable to me, too, yet I am compelled to believe. Your uncle packed a suitcase last night and left. I saw him go. He said goodbye to me. He put me in charge of his affairs and yours. Here are his instructions on that score."

Hall drew out his pocketbook and selected several sheets of paper in the unmistakable handwriting of Sergius Constantine.

"And here, also, is a note to you. He was in great haste, you know. Come in and read them at breakfast."

It was a depressing meal, Grunya taking nothing more than a cup of coffee, and Hall toying half-heartedly with an egg. The final convincing of Grunya was brought about by a telegram addressed to Hall. The fact that it was in cipher, and that he possessed the key, satisfied her, but did not diminish the mystery.

"*Shall let you hear from me from time to time,*" Hall translated it. "*Love to Grunya. Tell her you have my consent to marry her. The rest depends on her.*"

"By this telegram I hope to be able to keep track of his movements," Hall explained. "And now let us go and be married."

"While he is a hunted creature over the face of the earth? Never! Something must be done. We must do something. I thought you were going to destroy this nest of murderers. Destroy it, then, and save him."

"I can't explain everything to you," he said gently. "But this is part of the program for destroying them. I did not plan it this way, but it got beyond me. I can tell you this much, though. If your uncle can escape for a year he will be immune; he will never be endangered again. And I think he can avoid his pursuers for that long. In the meantime I shall do everything in my power to aid him, though his own instructions limit me, as, for instance, when he says that under no circumstances are the police to be called in."

"When the year is up, then I shall marry," was Grunya's final judgment.

"Very well. And in the meantime, today, are you going in to stop in the city, or will you remain here?"

"I am going in on the next train."

"So am I."

"Then we'll go in together," Grunya said, with the first faint hint of a smile that morning.

It proved a busy day for Hall. Parting from Grunya when town was reached, he devoted himself to Dragomiloff's affairs and instructions. The manager of S. Constantine & Co. was stubbornly suspicious of Hall, despite the letter he delivered to him in his employer's handwriting. And when Hall called up Grunya on the telephone to confirm him, the manager doubted that it was Constantine's niece at the other end of the wire. So Grunya was compelled to come in person and substantiate Hall's statements.

Following upon that he and Grunya lunched together, after

which, alone, he went to take possession of Dragomiloff's quarters. Certain that Grunya knew nothing about the rooms where the deaf mute presided, Hall had sounded her and found that he was right.

The deaf mute made little trouble. By talking straight to him so that he could watch the lips, Hall discovered that conversation was no more difficult than with an ordinary person. On the other hand, the mute was forced to write whatever he wished to communicate to Hall. Upon receiving the letter which Hall presented from Dragomiloff, the fellow immediately pressed it to his nose and sniffed long and carefully. Satisfied by this means of its genuineness, he accepted Hall as the temporary master of the place.

That evening Hall had three callers. The first, a rotund, bewhiskered, and genial person who gave the name of Burdwell, was one of the agents of the Bureau. By reference to the list of descriptions of the members, Hall identified him, though not by the name he had given.

"Your name is not Burdwell," Hall said.

"I know it," was the answer. "Perhaps you can tell me what is."

"I can. It is Thompson—Sylvanius Thompson."

"It sounds familiar," was the jolly response. "Perhaps you can tell me something more."

"You have been associated with the organization for five years. You were born in Toronto. You are forty-seven years old. You were professor of sociology at Barlington University, and you were forced to resign because your economic teachings offended the founder. You have carried out twelve commissions. Shall I name them for you?"

Sylvanius Thompson held up a warning hand.

"We do not mention such occurrences."

"We do in this room," Hall retorted.

The ex-professor of sociology immediately acknowledged the correctness of the statement.

"No use naming them all," he said. "Give me the first and the last, and I'll know I can talk business with you."

Again Hall referred to the list.

"Your first was Sig Lemuels, a police magistrate. It was your entrance test. Your last was Bertram Festle, who was supposed to have been drowned while going aboard his yacht at Bar Point."

"Very good." Sylvanius Thompson paused to light a cigar. "I merely wanted to make sure, that's all. I've never met anybody but the Chief here, so it was rather unprecedented to have to deal with a stranger. Now to business. I haven't had a commission for some time now, and funds are running low."

Hall drew out a typed copy he had made of Dragomiloff's instructions and read a certain paragraph carefully.

"There is nothing on hand now," he said. "But here is two thousand dollars with which to keep going. This is an advance on future services. Keep closely in touch, for you may be needed any time. The Bureau has a big affair on hand, and the assistance of all its members may be called for any time. In fact, I am empowered to tell you that the very life of the organization is at stake. Your receipt, please."

The ex-professor signed the receipt, puffed at his cigar, and evidenced no intention of going.

"Do you like to kill men?" Hall asked bluntly.

"Oh, I don't mind it," answered Thompson, "though I can't say that I like it. But one must live. I have a wife and three children."

"Do you believe your way of making a living is right?" was Hall's next question.

"Certainly; else I would not make my living that way. Besides, I am not a murderer. I am an executioner. No man is ever removed by the Bureau without cause—and by that I mean righteous cause. Only arch-offenders against society are removed, as you know yourself."

"I don't mind telling you, Professor, that I know very little about it. It is true, though I am in temporary charge of the Bureau and acting under most rigid instructions. Tell me, may you not place mistaken faith in the Chief?"

"I do not follow."

"I mean ethical faith. May he not be mistaken in his judgments? May he not select you, for instance, to kill—I beg pardon—to execute, a man who is not an arch-offender against society, or who may be entirely innocent of the misdeeds charged against him?"

"No, young man, that cannot happen. Whenever a commission is offered me—and I presume this is true of the other members—I first of all call for the evidence and weigh it carefully. I once even declined a certain commission because of reasonable doubt. It is true, I was afterwards proved wrong, but the principle was there, you see. Why, the Bureau could not last a year if it were not impregnably founded on right. I, for one, could not look my wife in the eyes nor take my innocent children in my arms did I believe it to be otherwise with the Bureau and the commissions I carry out for the Bureau."

Next, after the ex-professor, came Haas, livid and hungry-looking, to report progress.

"The Chief is headed towards Chicago," he began. "He ran his auto clear through to Albany and got away on the New York Central. His Pullman berth was for Chicago. I was too late to follow him, so I got a wire to Schwartz in the city here, who caught the next train. Also I telegraphed to the head of the Chicago Bureau—you know him?"

"Yes; Starkington."

"I telegraphed him, telling him the situation and to put a couple of members after the Chief. Then I came on to New York in order to get Harrison. The two of us leave for Chicago the first thing in the morning, if, in the meantime, no word comes from Starkington that they have got him."

"But you have exceeded your instructions," Hall objected. "I heard Drag—the Chief explicitly tell you that Schwartz and Harrison were to assist, and that the aid of the rest of the organization was to be called for only after the three of you had failed, and failed for a considerable time. You haven't failed yet. You have not even really begun."

"Evidently you know little about our system," Haas replied. "It has always been our custom when a chase leads to other cities to call upon any of the members who may be in those cities."

As Hall was about to speak, the deaf mute entered with a telegram addressed to Dragomiloff. Hall opened it and found it was from Starkington. He decoded it and then read it aloud to Haas.

"Has Haas gone crazy? Have received word from Haas that you appointed him to execute you, that you are headed for Chicago, and that I am to detail two members to fix you. Haas has never lied before. He must be crazy. He may prove dangerous. See to him."

"That is what Harrison said when I told him not an hour ago," was Haas's comment. "But I do not lie, and I am not crazy. You must fix this up, Mr. Hall."

Assisted by Haas, Hall composed a reply.

"Haas is neither lunatic nor liar. What he says is correct. Cooperate with him as requested.

               Winter Hall, Temporary Secretary."

"I'll send it myself," Haas said, as he rose to go.

A few minutes later Hall was telephoning to Grunya that her uncle was headed towards Chicago. This was followed by an interview with Harrison, who came privily to verify what Haas had told him, and who went away convinced.

Hall sat down alone to think things over. He glanced about at the book-cluttered walls and table, and the old feeling of unreality came over him. How could it be possible that there was an Assassination Bureau composed of ethical lunatics? And how could it be possible that he, who had set out to destroy this Assassination Bureau, was now actually managing it from its headquarters, and directing the pursuit and probable killing of the man who had created the Bureau, who was the father of the woman he loved, and whom he wished to save for his daughter's sake—how could it be possible?

And to prove that it was all true and real, a second telegram arrived from the head of the Chicago branch.

"Who in hell are you?" it demanded.

"Temporary acting secretary appointed by the Chief," was Hall's reply.

Hall was awakened from sleep several hours later by a third Chicago telegram.

"Everything too irregular. Decline further communication with you. Where is the Chief?

Starkington."

"Chief gone to Chicago. Watch incoming trains and get him to verify instructions to Haas. I don't care if you never communicate."

Hall flashed back.

By noon of next day Starkington's messages began to arrive thick and fast.

"Have met Chief. He verifies everthing. Accept my apology. He broke my arm and got away. Have commissioned the four Chicago members to get him."

"Schwartz has just arrived."

"Think Chief may head west. Am wiring St. Louis, Denver, and San Francisco to watch for him. This may prove expensive. Forward money for contingencies."

"Dempsey has three broken ribs and right arm paralyzed. Paralysis not permanent. Chief got away."

"Chief is still in Chicago but cannot locate him."

"St. Louis, Denver, and San Francisco have replied. They tell me I am crazy. Will you please verify?"

This last wire had been preceded by messages from the three mentioned cities, all incredulous of Starkington's sanity, and Hall had replied to them as he originally replied to Starkington.

It was while this muddle was pending that Hall, struck by an idea, sent a long telegram to Starkington and made a still greater muddle.

"Stop pursuit of Chief. Call a conference of Chicago members and consider following proposition. Judgment of execution of Chief irregular. Chief passed judgment on himself. Why? He must be crazy. It will not be right to kill one who has done no wrong. What wrong has Chief done? Where is your sanction?"

That this was a poser, and that it stopped Chicago's hand, was proved by the reply.

"Have talked it over. You are right. Chief's judgment on self invalid. Chief has done no wrong. Shall leave him alone. Dempsey's arm is better. All are agreed that Chief must be crazy."

Hall was jubilant. He had played these ethical madmen to the top of their madness. Dragomiloff was safe. That evening he took Grunya to the theatre and to supper and encouraged her with sanguine hopes for her uncle. But on his return home he found a sheaf of telegrams awaiting him.

"Have received wire from Chicago calling off Chief deal. Your last wire contradicts this. What are we to conclude?
St. Louis."

"Chicago now cancels orders against Chief. By our rules no order ever canceled. What is the matter?

Denver."

"Where is Chief? Why doesn't he communicate with us? Chicago by latest wire has receded from earlier position. Is everybody crazy? Or is it a joke?

San Francisco."

"Chief still in Chicago. Met Carthey on State Street. Tried to entice Carthey into following him. Then followed Carthey and reproached him. Carthey said nothing doing. Chief very angry. Insists killing order be carried out.

Starkington."

"Chief encountered Carthey later. Committed unprovoked assault on Carthey. Carthey not injured.

Starkington."

"Chief called on me. Upbraided me bitterly. Told him your message had changed our minds. Chief furious. Is he crazy?

Starkington."

"Your interference is spoiling everything. What right have you to interfere? This must be rectified. What are you trying to do? Reply.

Drago."

"Trying to do the right thing. You cannot violate your own rules. Members have no sanction to perform act."

was Hall's reply.

"Bosh."

was Dragomiloff's last word for the night.

8

It was not till eleven on the following morning that Hall received word of Dragomiloff's next play. It came from the Chief himself.

"Have sent this message to all branches. Have given it in person to Chicago branch which will verify. I believe that our organization is wrong. I believe all its work has been wrong. I believe every member, wittingly or not, to be wrong. Consider this your sanction and do your duty."

Soon the verdicts of the branches began to pour in on Hall, who smiled as he forwarded them to Dragomiloff. One and all were agreed that no reason had been advanced for taking the Chief's life.

"A belief is not a sin," said New Orleans.

"It is not incorrectness of a belief but insincerity of a belief that makes a crime," was Boston's contribution to the symposium.

"Chief's honest belief is no wrong," concluded St. Louis.

"Ethical disagreement does not constitute any sanction whatever," announced Denver.

While San Francisco flippantly remarked, "The only thing for the Chief to do is to retire from control or forget it."

Dragomiloff replied by sending out another general message. It ran:

"My belief is about to take form of deeds. Believing organization to be wrong, I shall stamp out organization. I shall personally destroy members, and if necessary shall have recourse to the police. Chicago will verify this to all branches. I shall shortly afford even stronger sanction for branches to proceed against me."

Hall waited for the replies with keen interest, confessing to himself his inability to forecast what this society of righteous madmen would conclude next. It turned out to be a division of opinion. Thus San Francisco:

"Sanction O.K. Await instructions."

Denver advised:

"Recommend Chicago branch examine Chief's sanity. We have good sanatoriums up here."

New Orleans complained:

"Is everybody crazy? We are without sufficient data. Will somebody straighten this matter out?"

Said Boston:

"In this crisis we must keep our heads. Perhaps Chief is ill. This must be ascertained satisfactorily before any decision is reached."

It was after this that Starkington wired to suggest that Haas, Schwartz, and Harrison be returned to New York. To this Hall agreed, but hardly had he got the telegram off, when a later one from Starkington changed the complexion of the situation.

"Carthey has just been murdered. Police looking for slayer but have no clues. It is our belief that Chief is responsible. Please forward to all branches."

Hall, as the focal communicating point of the branches, was now fairly swamped in a sea of telegrams. Twenty-four hours later Chicago had even more startling information.

"Schwartz throttled at three this afternoon. There is no doubt this time of Chief. Police are pursuing him. So are we. Has dropped from sight. All branches be on the lookout. It means trouble. Am proceeding without sanction of branches, but should like same."

And promptly the sanctions poured in on Hall. Dragomiloff had achieved his purpose. At last the ethical madmen were aroused and after him.

Hall himself was in a quandary, and cursed his ethical nature that made him value a promise. He was convinced, now, that Dragomiloff was really a lunatic, having burst forth from his quiet book-and-business life and become a homicidal maniac. That he had promised a maniac various things brought up the question whether or not, ethically, he was justified in breaking those promises. His common sense told him that he was justified—justified in informing the police, justified in bringing about the arrests of all the members of the Assassination Bureau, justified in anything that promised to put a stop to the orgy of killing that seemed impending. But above his common sense was his ethics, and at times he was convinced that he was as mad as any of the madmen with whom he dealt.

To add to his perplexity, Grunya, who managed to get his

address from the telephone number he had given her, paid him a call.

"I have come to say goodbye," was her introduction. "What comfortable rooms you have. And what a curious servant. He never spoke a word to me."

"Goodbye?" Hall queried. "Are you going back to Edge Moor?"

She shook her head and smiled airily.

"No; Chicago. I am going to find Uncle, and to help him if I can. What last word have you received? Is he still in Chicago?"

"By the last word . . ." Hall hesitated. "Yes, by the last word he had not left Chicago. But you can't be of any help, and it is unwise of you to go."

"I'm going just the same."

"Let me advise you, dear."

"Not until the year is up—except in business matters. In fact I came to turn my little affairs over to you. I go on the Twentieth Century this afternoon."

Argument with Grunya was useless, but Hall was too sensible to quarrel, and parted from her in appropriate lover fashion, remaining in the headquarters of the Assassination Bureau to manage its lunatic affairs.

Nothing happened of moment for another twenty-four hours. Then it came, an avalanche of messages, precipitated by one from Starkington.

"Chief still here. Broke Harrison's neck today. Police do not connect case with Schwartz. Please call for help on all branches."

Hall sent out this general call, and an hour later received the following from Starkington:

"Broke into hospital and killed Dempsey. Has definitely left city. Haas in pursuit. St. Louis take warning."

"Rastenaff and Pillsworthy start immediately," Boston informed Hall.

"Lucoville has been dispatched to Chicago," said New Orleans.

"Not sending anybody. Are waiting for Chief to arrive," St. Louis advised.

And then Grunya's Chicago wail:

"Have you any later news?"

He did not answer this, but very shortly received a second from her.

"Do please help me if you have heard."

Hall replied:

"Has left Chicago. Probably heading towards St. Louis. Let me join you."

And to this, in turn, he received no answer, and was left to contemplate the flight of the Chief of the Assassins, pursued by his daughter and the assassins of four cities, and heading towards the nest of assassins waiting in St. Louis.

Another day went by, and another. The van of pursuers arrived in St. Louis, but there was no sign of Dragomiloff. Haas was reported missing. Grunya could find no trace of her uncle. Only the head of the branch remained in Boston, and he informed Hall that he would follow if anything further happened. In Chicago there was left only Starkington with his broken arm.

But at the end of another forty-eight hours, Dragomiloff struck again. Rastenaff and Pillsworthy had arrived in St. Louis in the early morning. Each, perforated by a small-calibre bullet, had been carried from his Pullman berth by men sent from the coroner's office. The two St. Louis members were likewise dead. The head of that branch, the only survivor, sent the information. Haas had reappeared, but no explanation of his four days' disappearance was vouchsafed. Dragomiloff had again dropped out of sight. Grunya was inconsolable and bombarded Hall with telegrams. The head of the Boston branch sent word that he had started. And so did Starkington, despite his injury. San Francisco was of the opinion that Denver would be the Chief's next point, and sent two men there to reinforce; while Denver, of the same opinion, kept her two men in readiness.

All this made big inroads on the emergency fund of the Bureau, and it was with satisfaction that Hall, adhering to his instructions, wired sum after sum of money to the different men. If the pace were kept up, he decided, the Bureau would be bankrupt before the end of the year.

And then came a slack period. All members having gone to the West, and being in touch with each other there, nothing was left for Hall to do. He endured the suspense and idleness for a day or so; then, making financial arrangements and arranging with the deaf mute for the forwarding of telegrams, he closed up the headquarters of the Bureau and bought a ticket for St. Louis.

9

In St. Louis, Hall found no change in the situation. Dragomiloff had not reappeared and everybody was waiting for something to happen. Hall attended a conference at Murgweather's house. Murgweather was the head of the St. Louis branch, and lived with his family in a comfortable suburban bungalow. All were gathered when Hall arrived, and he immediately recognized Haas, the lean flame of a man, and Starkington he knew by the arm in splints and sling.

"Who is the man?" demanded Lucoville, the New Orleans member, when Hall was being introduced.

"Temporary Secretary of the Bureau," Murgweather started to explain.

"It is entirely too irregular to suit me," Lucoville snapped back. "He is not one of us. He has killed no man. He has passed no test of the organization. Not only is his appearance among us unprecedented, but for men who pursue such a hazardous vocation as ours his presence is a menace. And in connection with this, I wish to point out two things. First, by reputation he is known to all of us. I have nothing derogatory to say about his work in the world. I have read his books with interest, and, I may add, profit. His contributions to sociology have been distinct and distinctive. On the other hand, though, he is a socialist. He is called the 'Millionaire Socialist.' What does that mean? It means that he is out of touch with us and our principles of conduct. It means that he is a blind creature of Law. Law is his fetish. He grovels in the mire of ignorance and worships Law. To him, we, who are above the Law, are arch-offenders against the Law. Therefore, his presence bodes no good for us. He is bound to destroy us for the sake of his fetish. This is only in the nature of things. This is the dictate of both his personal and his philosophical temperament.

"And secondly, notice that of all times, it is in this time of crisis to the organization that he has chosen to intrude. Who has vouched for him? Who has admitted him to our secrets? Only one man, and that man the Chief, the one who is now bent on destroying us, who has already killed six of our members and who threatens to expose us to the police. This looks bad, very bad, for him and us. He is the enemy within our ranks. It is my suggestion that we put him away—"

"Pardon me, my dear Lucoville," Murgweather interrupted. "This discussion is out of order. Mr. Hall is my guest."

"All our heads are in the noose," retorted the member from New Orleans. "And guest or no guest, this is no time for social amenities. The man is a spy. He is bent on destroying us. I charge him with it in his presence. What has he to say?"

Hall glanced around at the circle of suspicious faces, and, with the exception of Lucoville, he noted that none was angry. In truth, he decided, they were mad philosophers.

Murgweather made a vain effort to interpose, but was overruled.

"What have you to say, Mr. Hall?" Hanover, the head of the Boston branch, demanded.

"If I may sit down, I shall be glad to reply," was Hall's answer.

Apologies were rendered all around, and he was ensconced in a big armchair that was drawn up to form one of the circle.

"My reply, like the charges, will be under two heads," he began. "In the first place, I *am* bent on destroying your organization."

This declaration was received in courteous silence, and the thought came into Hall's mind that as philosophers and madmen they were certainly consistent. Emotion of every sort was absent from their faces. They waited at scholarly attention for the rest of his discourse. Even Lucoville's flash of anger had been momentary, and he now sat as composed as the rest.

"Why I am bent on destroying your organization is too big a subject to open at this moment," Hall continued. "I may say, in passing, that it is I who am responsible for your Chief's changed conduct. When I discovered what an extreme ethicist he was, and each of the rest of you, I gave him fifty thousand dollars to accept a commission against himself. I furnished him with a sanction, ethical, of course, and the execution of the commission he turned over to Mr. Haas in my presence. Am I right, Mr. Haas?"

"You are."

"And in my presence, the Chief informed you of my secretaryship. Am I right?"

"You are."

"Now I come to the second head. Why did the Chief trust me with the headquarters management of the Bureau? The answer is simply and directly to the point. He knew that I was at least halfway as ethically mad as the rest of you. He knew that it was impossible for me to break my word. This I have proved by my subsequent actions. I have done my best to fulfill the office of acting secretary. I have forwarded all telegrams, general calls, and orders. I have granted all requests for funds. I shall continue to do as I have agreed, though I hold in detestation and horror, ethically, all that you stand for. I am doing what I believe to be right. Am I right?"

The pause that followed was very slight. Lucoville arose, walked over to him, and gravely extended his hand. The others did the same. Then Starkington preferred a request that adequate provision be made from the funds of the Bureau for the support of Dempsey's widow and of Harrison's widow and children. There was little discussion, and when the sums were decided upon, Hall wrote the checks and turned them over to Murgweather to be forwarded.

The question next taken up was that of the crisis and of how best to cope with the recreant Chief. In this Hall took no part, so that, lying back in his chair, he was able to observe and study these curious madmen. There were seven of them, and, with the exceptions of Haas and Lucoville, they had all the appearance of middle-aged, middle-class, scholarly gentlemen. He could not bring himself to realize that they were cold-blooded murderers, assassins for hire. And by the same token, it was incredible that they who were so calm should be the survivors of the deadly war that was being waged against them. Half of their number were already dead. Hanover was the sole survivor of Boston, Haas of New York, Starkington of Chicago, and their genial and bewhiskered host, Murgweather, of St. Louis.

"I enjoyed your last book," Hall's host leaned over and whispered to him in an interval. "Your argument for organization by industry as against organization by craft was unimpeachable. But to my notion, your exposition of the law of diminishing returns was rather lame. I have a bone to pick with you there."

And this man was an assassin!—all these men were assassins! Hall could believe only by accepting them as lunatics. And going into town on the electric car after the meeting, he sat and talked with Haas, and was astounded to find him an ex-professor of Greek and Hebrew. Lucoville proved to be an expert in Oriental research. Hanover, he learned, had once been headmaster of one of the most select New England academies, while Starkington turned out to be an ex-newspaper editor of no mean reputation.

"But why have you, for instance, gone in for this mode of life?" Hall asked.

They were sitting on the outside of the car, which had arrived in the hotel district. The theatres were just letting out, and the sidewalks were crowded.

"Because it is right," Haas answered, "and because it is a better means of livelihood than Greek and Hebrew. If I had my life all over again—"

But Hall was never to hear the end of that sentence. The car was stopped at a crossing for a moment, and Haas was suddenly electrified by something he had seen. With a flash of eye, and without a word or motion of farewell, he sprang from the car and was lost to view in the moving crowd.

Next morning Hall understood. In the paper was a sensational account of a mysterious attempt at murder. Haas was lying at the receiving hospital with a perforated lung. The doctors' examination showed that he owed his life to an abnormal, misplaced heart. Had his heart been where it ought to have been, said the report, the bullet or missile would have passed through it. But this did not constitute the mystery. No one had heard the shot fired. Haas had suddenly slumped in the midst of a thick crowd. A woman, pressed against him in the jam, testified that at the moment before he fell she heard a faint, though sharp, metallic click. A man, in front of him, though he had heard the click but was not sure.

"The police are mystified," the newspaper said. "The victim, a stranger in the city, is equally mystified. He claims to know of no person or persons who might be liable to seek his life. Nor does he remember having heard the click. He was aware only of a violent impact as the strange missile entered. Sergeant of Detectives O'Connell believes the weapon to have been an air-rifle, but this is denied by Chief of Detectives Randall, who claims to know air-rifles, who denies that such a weapon could be utilized unseen in a dense crowd."

"It was the Chief without doubt," Murgweather was assuring Hall a few minutes later. "He is still in town. Will you please inform Denver, San Francisco, and New Orleans of the event? The weapon is the Chief's own invention. Several times he has loaned it to Harrison, who always returned it after using. The compressed-air chamber is strapped on the body under the arm or wherever is most convenient. The discharging mechanism is no larger than a toy pistol, and can be readily concealed in the hand. We must be very careful from now on."

"I am in no danger," Hall answered. "I am only Temporary Secretary, and am not a member."

"I am glad that Haas will recover," Murgweather said. "He is a very estimable man and a scholar. I have the keenest appreciation of his intellect, though he is prone to be too serious at times, and, I fear me, finds a certain pleasure in taking human life."

"Don't you?" Hall asked quickly.

"No, and no other one of us, with the exception of Haas. He has the temperament for it. Believe me, Mr. Hall, though I have faithfully performed my tasks for the Bureau, and despite my ethical convictions as to the righteousness of the acts, I never put through an execution without qualms of the flesh. I know it is foolish, but I cannot overcome it. Why, I was positively nauseated by my first affair. I have written a monograph upon the subject, not for publication, of course, but it is a very interesting field of study. If you care to, I shall be glad for you to come out to the house some evening and glance over what I have written."

"Thank you, I shall."

"It is a curious problem," Murgweather continued. "The sacredness of human life is a social concept. The primitive natural man never had any qualms about killing his fellow man. Theoretically, I should have none. Yet I do have. The question is: how do they arise? Has the long evolution to civilization impressed this concept into the cerebral cells of the race? Or is it due to my training in childhood and adolescence, before I became an emancipated thinker? Or may it not be due to both causes? It is very curious."

"I am sure it is," Hall answered dryly. "But what are you going to do about the Chief?"

"Kill him. It is all we can do, and we certainly must assert our right to live. The situation is a new one to us, however. Hitherto, the men we destroyed were unaware of their danger. Also, they never pursued us. But the Chief does know our intention, and, furthermore, he is destroying us. We have never been hunted before. He has certainly been more fortunate than we. But I must be going. I agreed to meet Hanover at quarter past."

"But aren't you afraid?" Hall asked.

"Of what?"

"Of the Chief killing you?"

"No; it won't matter much. You see, I am well insured, and in my own experience I have exploded one generally accepted notion, namely, that the man who has taken many lives is, by those very acts, made more afraid himself to die. This is not true. I have demonstrated it. The more I have administered death to others—eighteen times, by my count—the easier death has seemed to me. Those very qualms I spoke of are the qualms of life. They belong to life, not to death. I have written a few detached thoughts on the subject. If you care to glance at them . . ."

"Yes, indeed," Hall assured him.

"This evening, then. Say at eleven. If I am detained by this affair, ask to be shown into my study. I'll lay the manuscript, and that of the monograph, too, on the reading table for you. I'd prefer to read them aloud and discuss them with you, but if I can't be there, jot down any notes of criticism that may come to you."

10

"I know there is much you are concealing from me, and I cannot understand why. Surely, you are not unwilling to aid me in saving Uncle Sergius?"

Grunya's last sentence was uttered pleadingly, and her eyes were warm with the golden glow that for this once failed to reach Hall's heart.

"Uncle Sergius doesn't seem to need much saving," he muttered grimly.

"Now just what do you mean?" she cried, quickly suspicious.

"Nothing, nothing, I assure you, except merely that he has escaped so far."

"But how do you know he has escaped?" she insisted. "May he not be dead? He has not been heard of since he left Chicago. How do you know but what those brutes have killed him?"

"He has been seen here in St. Louis—"

"There!" she interrupted excitedly. "I knew you were keeping things from me! Now, honestly, aren't you?"

"I am," Hall confessed. "But by your uncle's own instructions. Believe me, you cannot be of the least assistance to him. You can't even find him. It would be wise for you to return to New York."

For an hour longer she catechized him and he wasted advice on her, and they parted in mutual irritation.

Promptly at eleven, Hall rang the bell at Murgweather's bungalow. A little sleepy-eyed maidservant of fourteen or fifteen, apparently aroused from bed, admitted and led him to Murgweather's study.

"He's in there," she said, pushing open the door and leaving him.

At the further side of the room, seated at the table, partly in the light of a reading lamp, but more in shadow, was Murgweather. His crossed arms rested on the table, and on them rested his bowed head. Evidently asleep, Hall concluded, as he crossed over. He spoke to him, then touched him on the shoulder, but there was no response. He felt the genial assassin's hand and found it cold. A stain upon the floor, and a perforation of the reading jacket beneath the shoulder, told the story. Murgweather's heart had been in the right place. An open window, directly behind, showed how the deed had been accomplished.

Hall drew the heap of manuscript from beneath the dead man's arms. He had been killed as he pored over what he had written. "Some Casual Thoughts on Death," Hall read the title, then searched on till he found the monograph, "A Tentative Explanation of Certain Curious Psychological Traits."

It would never do for Murgweather's family if such damning evidence were found with the corpse, was Hall's decision. He burned them in the fireplace, turned down the lamp, and crept softly out of the house.

Early the following morning, the news was broken to him in his room by Starkington, but it was not until afternoon that the papers published the account. Hall was frightened. The little maidservant had been interviewed, and that she had used her sleepy eyes to some purpose was shown by the excellence of the description she gave of the visitor she had admitted at eleven o'clock the previous night. The detail she gave was almost photographic. Hall got up abruptly and looked at himself in the glass. There was no mistaking it. The reflection he saw was precisely that of the man for whom the police were searching. Even to the scarf-pin, he was that man.

He made a hurried rummage of his luggage and arrayed himself as dissimilarly as possible. Then, dodging into a taxi from the side entrance of the hotel, he made the round of the shops, from headgear to footgear purchasing a new outfit.

Back at the hotel, he found he had just time to catch a westbound train. Fortunately, he was able to get Grunya to the telephone, so as to tell her of his departure. Also, he took the liberty of guessing that Dragomiloff's next appearance would be in Denver, and he advised her to follow on.

Once on the train and out of the city, he breathed more easily, and was able more calmly to consider the situation. He, too, he decided, was on the adventure path, and a madly tangled path it was. Starting out with the intention of running down the Assassination Bureau and destroying it, he had fallen in love with the daughter of its organizer, become Temporary Secretary of the Bureau, and was now being sought by the police for the murder of one of the members who had been killed by the Chief of the Bureau. "No more practical sociology for me," he said to himself. "When I get out of this I shall confine myself to theory. Closet sociology from now on."

At the depot in Denver, he was greeted sadly by Harkins, the head of the local branch. Not until they were in a machine and whirling uptown did the cause of Harkins's sadness come out.

"Why didn't you warn us?" he said reproachfully. "You let him give you the slip, and we were so certain that his account would be settled in St. Louis that we were not prepared."

"He has arrived, then?"

"Arrived? Gracious! The first we knew, two of us were done for—Bostwick, who was like a brother to me, and Calkins, of San Francisco. And now Harding, the other San Francisco man, has dropped from sight. It is terrible." He paused and shuddered. "I parted from Bostwick not more than fifteen minutes before it happened. He was so bright and cheerful. And now his little love-saturated home! His dear wife is inconsolable."

Tears ran down Harkins's cheeks, so blinding him that he slowed the pace of the machine. Hall was curious. Here was a new type of madman, a sentimental assassin.

"But why should it be terrible?" he queried. "You have dealt death to others. It is the same phenomenon in all cases."

"But this is different. He was my friend, my comrade."

"Possibly others that you have killed had friends and comrades."

"But if you could have seen him in his little home," Harkins maundered on. "He was a model husband and father. He was a good man, an excellently good man, a saint, so considerate that he would not harm a fly."

"But what happened to him was only what he had made happen to others," Hall objected.

"No, no; it is different!" the other cried passionately. "If you had only known him. To know him was to love him. Everybody loved him."

"Undoubtedly his victims as well?"

"Aye, had they had the opportunity they could not have helped loving him," Harkins proclaimed vehemently. "If you only knew the good he has done and was continually doing. His four-footed friends loved him. The very flowers loved him. He was president of the Humane Society. He was the strongest worker among the anti-vivisectionists. He was in himself a whole society for the prevention of cruelty to animals."

"Bostwick . . . Charles N. Bostwick," Hall murmured. "Yes, I remember. I have noticed some of his magazine articles."

"Who does not know him?" Harkins broke in ecstatically, and broke off long enough to blow his nose. "He was a great power for good, a great power for good. I would gladly change places with him right now, to have him back in the world."

Nevertheless, outside of his love for Bostwick, Hall found Harkins to be a keen, intelligent man. He stopped the machine at a telegraph office.

"I told them to hold any messages for me this morning," he explained as he got out.

In a minute he was back, and together, with the aid of the

cipher, they translated the telegram he had received. It was from Harding, and had been sent from Ogden.

"Westbound," it ran. "Chief on board. Am waiting opportunity. Shall succeed."

"He won't," Hall volunteered. "The Chief will get Harding."

"Harding is a strong and alert man," Harkins affirmed.

"I tell you, you fellows don't realize what you're up against."

"We realize that the life of the organization is at stake, and that we must deal with a recreant Chief."

"If you thoroughly realized the situation you'd head for tall timber and climb a tree and let the organization go smash."

"But that would be wrong," Harkins protested gravely.

Hall threw up his hands in despair.

"To make it doubly sure," the other continued, "I shall immediately tell the comrades at St. Louis to come on. If Harding fails—"

"Which he will."

"We'll proceed to San Francisco. In the meantime—"

"In the meantime, you'll please run me back to the depot," Hall interrupted, glancing at his watch. "There's a westbound train due. I'll met you in San Francisco, at the St. Francis Hotel, if you don't meet the Chief first. If you do meet him first . . . well, it's goodbye now and for good."

Before the train started, Hall had time to write a note to Grunya, which Harkins was to deliver to her on the train. The note informed her of her uncle's continued westward flight and advised her, when she got to San Francisco, to register at the Fairmont Hotel.

11

At Reno, Nevada, a dispatch was delivered to Hall. It was from the sentimental Denver assassin.

"Man ground to pieces at Winnemucca. Must be Chief. Return at once. Members all arriving Denver. We must reorganize."

But Hall grinned and remained on his westbound train. The reply he wired was:

"Better identify. Did you deliver letter to lady?"

Three days later, at the St. Francis Hotel, Hall heard again from the manager of the Denver Bureau. This wire was from Winnemucca, Nevada.

"My mistake. It was Harding. Chief surely heading for San Francisco. Inform local branch. Am following. Delivered letter. Lady remained on train."

But no trace of Grunya could Hall find in San Francisco. Nor could Breen and Alsworthy, the two local members, help him. Hall even went over to Oakland and ferreted out the sleeping car she had arrived in and the Negro porter of the car. She had come to San Francisco and promptly disappeared.

The assassins began to string in—Hanover of Boston, Haas, the hungry one with the misplaced heart, Starkington of Chicago, Lucoville of New Orleans, John Gray of New Orleans, and Harkins of Denver. With the two San Francisco members there was a total of eight. They were all that survived in the United States. As was well known to them, Hall did not count. While Temporary Secretary of the organization, disbursing its funds and transmitting its telegrams, he was not one of them and his life was not threatened by the mad leader.

What convinced Hall that they were all madmen was the uniform kindness with which they treated him and the confidence they reposed in him. They knew him to be the original cause of their troubles; they knew he was bent upon the destruction of the Assassination Bureau and that he had furnished the fifty thousand dollars for the death of their Chief; and yet they gave Hall credit for what he considered the rightness of his conduct and for the particular streak of ethical madness that simmered somewhere in his make-up and compelled him to play fairly with them. He did not betray them. He handled their funds honestly; and he performed satisfactorily all the duties of Temporary Secretary.

With the exception of Haas, who, despite his achievements in Greek and Hebrew, was too kin to the tiger in lust to kill, Hall could not help but like these learned lunatics who had made a fetish of ethics and who took the lives of fellow humans with the same coolness and directness of purpose with which they solved problems in mathematics, made translations of hieroglyphics, or carried through chemical analyses in the test-tubes of their laboratories. John Gray he liked most of all. A quiet Englishman, in appearance and carriage a country squire, John Gray entertained radical ideas concerning the function of the drama. During the weeks of waiting, when there was no sign of Dragomiloff or Grunya, Gray and Hall frequented the theatres together, and to Hall their friendship proved a liberal education. During this period, Lucoville became immersed in basketry, devoting himself in particular to the recurrent triple-fish design so common in the baskets of the Ukiah Indians. Harkins painted water colors, after the Japanese school, of leaves, mosses, grasses, and ferns. Breen, a bacteriologist, continued his search of years for the parasite of the corn-worm. Alsworthy's hobby was wireless telephony, and he and Breen divided an attic laboratory between them. And Hanover, an immediate patron of the city's libraries, surrounded himself with scientific books and worked at the fourteenth chapter of a ponderous tome which he had entitled *Physical Compulsions of the Aesthetics of Color.* He put Hall to sleep one warm afternoon by reading to him the first and thirteenth chapters.

The two months of inaction would not have occurred, and the assassins would have gone back to their home cities, had it not been for the fact that they were baited to remain by a weekly message from Dragomiloff. Regularly, each Saturday night, Alsworthy was called up by telephone, and over the wire heard the unmistakable toneless and colorless voice of the Chief. He always reiterated the one suggestion that the surviving members of the Assassination Bureau disband the organization. Hall, present at one of their councils, seconded the proposition. The hearing they accorded him was out of courtesy only, for he was not one of them; and he stood alone in the opinion he expressed.

As they saw it, there was no possible way by which they could break their oaths. The rules of the Bureau had never been broken. Even Dragomiloff had not broken them. In strict accord with the rules he had accepted Hall's fee of fifty thousand dollars, judged himself and his acts as socially hurtful, passed sentence on himself, and selected Haas to execute the sentence. Who were they, they demanded, that they should behave less rightly than their Chief? To disband an organization which they believed socially justifiable would be a monstrous wrong. As Lucoville said, "It would stultify all morality and place us on the level of the beasts. Are we beasts?"

And "No! No! No!" had been the passionate cries of the members.

"Madmen yourselves," Hall called them. "As mad as your Chief is mad."

"All moralists have been considered mad," Breen retorted. "Or, to be precise, have been considered mad by the common ruck of their times. No moralist, unworthy of contempt, can act contrary to his belief. All crucifixions and martyrdoms have been gladly accepted by the true moralists. It was the only way to give power to their teaching. Faith! That's it! And, as the slang of the day goes, they delivered the goods. They had faith in the right they envisioned. What is the life of man compared with the living truth of the thought of man? A vain thing is precept without example. Are we preceptors who dare not be exemplars?"

"No! No! No!" had been the chorus of approbation.

"We dare not, as true thinkers and right-livers, by thought, much less by deed, negate the high principles we expound," said Harkins.

"Nor can we otherwise climb upwards towards the light," Hanover added.

"We are not madmen," Alsworthy cried. "We are men who see clearly. We are high priests at the altar of right conduct. As well call our good friend, Winter Hall, a madman. If truth be mad, and we are touched by it, is not Winter Hall likewise touched? He has called us ethical lunatics. What else, then, has his conduct been but ethical lunacy? Why has he not denounced us to the police? Why does he, holding our views abhorrent, continue to act as our Secretary? He is not even bound by solemn contracts as we are. He merely bowed his head and consented to do the several things requested of him by our recreant Chief. He belongs to both sides in the present controversy; the Chief trusts him; we trust him; and he betrays neither one side nor the other. We know and like him. I, for one, find but two things distasteful in him: first, his sociology, and, second, his desire to destroy our organization. But when it comes to ethics he is as like us as a pea in a pod is to its fellows."

"I, too, am touched," Hall murmured sadly. "I admit it. I confess it. You are such likable lunatics, and I am so weak, or strong, or foolish, or wise—I don't know what—that I cannot break my given word. All the same, I wish I could bring you fellows to my way of thinking, as I brought the Chief to my way of thinking."

"Oh, but did you?" Lucoville cried. "Why then did the Chief not retire from the organization?"

"Because he had accepted the fee I paid for his life," Hall answered.

"And for the same reasons precisely are we plighted to take his life," Lucoville drove the point home. "Are we less moral than our Chief? By our compacts, when the Chief accepted the fee we were bound to carry into execution his agreement with you. It mattered not what that agreement might be. It chanced to be the Chief's own death." He shrugged his shoulders. "What would you? The Chief must die, else we are not exemplars of what we believe to be right."

"There you go, always harking back to morality," Hall complained.

"And why not?" Lucoville concluded grandly. "The world is founded on morality. Without morality the world would perish. There is a righteousness in the elements themselves. Destroy morality and you would destroy gravitation. The very rocks would fly apart. The whole sidereal system would fume into the unthinkableness of chaos."

12

One evening, at the Poodle Dog Café, Hall waited vainly for John Gray to join him at dinner. The theatre, as usual, had been planned for afterwards. But John Gray did not come, and by half past eight Hall returned to the St. Francis Hotel, under his arm a bundle of current magazines, intent on early to bed. There was something familiar about the walk of the woman who preceded him towards the elevator, and, with a quick intake of breath, he hurried after.

"Grunya," he said softly, as the elevator started.

In one instant she gave him a startled glance from trouble-burdened eyes, and the next instant she had caught his hand between both of hers and was clinging to it as if for strength.

"Oh, Winter," she breathed. "Is it you? That is why I came to the St. Francis. I thought I might find you. I need you so. Uncle Sergius is mad, quite mad. He ordered me to pack up for a long journey. We sail tomorrow. He compelled me to leave the house and to come to a downtown hotel, promising to join me later, or to join me on the steamer tomorrow morning. I engaged rooms for him. But something is going to happen. He has some terrible plan in mind, I know. He—"

"What floor, sir?" the elevator operator interrupted.

"Go down again," Hall ordered, for there was no one else in the car.

"Wait," he cautioned. "We will go to the Palm Room and talk."

"No, no," she cried. "Let us get out on the street. I want to

walk. I want fresh air. I want to be able to think. Do you think
I am mad, Winter? Look at me. Do I look it?"

"Hush," he commanded, pressing her arm. "Wait. We will
talk it over. Wait."

It was patent that she was in a state of high excitement, and
her effort to control herself on the down-trip of the elevator was
successful but pitiful.

"Why didn't you communicate with me?" he asked, when
they had gained the sidewalk and were walking to the corner of
Powell, where he intended directing their course across Union
Square. "What became of you when you reached San Francisco?
You received my message at Denver. Why didn't you come to
the St. Francis?"

"I haven't time to tell you," she hurried on. "My head is
bursting. I don't know what to believe. It seems all a dream.
Such things are not possible. Uncle's mind is deranged. Sometimes I am absolutely sure there is no such thing as the Assassination Bureau. It is an imagining of Uncle Sergius. You, too,
have imagined it. This is the twentieth century. Such an awful
thing cannot be. I . . . I sometimes wonder if I have had typhoid
fever, or if I am not even now in the delirium of fever, with
nurses and doctors around me, raving all this nightmare myself.
Tell me, tell me, are you, too, a sprite of fantasy—a vision of a
disease-stricken brain?"

"No," he said gravely and slowly. "You are awake and well.
You are yourself. You are now crossing Powell Street with me.
The pavement is slippery. Do you not feel it underfoot? See
those tire chains on that motorcar. Your arm is in mine. This is
a real fog drifting across from the Pacific. Those are real people
on yonder benches. You see this beggar, asking me for money.
He is real. See, I give him a real half-dollar. He will most likely
spend it on real whiskey. I smelled his breath. Did you? It was
real, I assure you, very real. And we are real. Please grasp that.
Now, what is your trouble? Tell me all."

"Is there truly an organization of assassins?"

"Yes," he answered.

"How do you know? Is it not mere conjecture? May you not be inoculated with uncle's madness?"

Hall shook his head sadly. "I wish I were. Unfortunately, I know otherwise."

"How do you know?" she cried, pressing the fingers of her free hand wildly to her temple.

"Because I am Temporary Secretary of the Assassination Bureau."

She recoiled from him, half withdrawing her arm from his and being restrained only by a reassuring pressure on his part.

"You are one of the band of murderers that is trying to kill Uncle Sergius!"

"No; I am not one of the band. I merely have charge of its funds. Has you—er—your Uncle Sergius told you anything about the—er—the band?"

"Oh, endless ravings. He is so deranged that he believes that he organized it."

"He did," Hall said firmly. "He is crazy, there is no doubt of that; but nevertheless he made the Assassination Bureau and directed it."

Again she recoiled and strove to withdraw her arm.

"And will you next admit that it is you who paid the Bureau fifty thousand dollars in advance for his death?" she demanded.

"It is true. I admit it."

"How could you?" she moaned.

"Listen, Grunya, dear," he begged. "You have not heard all. You do not understand. At the time I paid the fee I did not know he was your father—"

He broke off abruptly, appalled at the slip he had made.

"Yes," she said, with growing calmness, "he told me he was my father, too. I took it for so much raving. Go on."

"Well, then, I did not know he was your father; nor did I know he was insane. Afterwards, when I learned, I pleaded with him. But he is mad. So are they all, all mad. And he is up to some new madness right now. You dread that something is going to happen. Tell me what are your suspicions. We may be able to prevent it."

"Listen!" She pressed close to him and spoke quickly in a low, controlled voice. "There is much explanation needed from both of us and to both of us. But first to the danger. When I arrived in San Francisco, why I do not know save that I had a presentiment, I went first to the morgue, then I made the round of the hospitals. And I found him, in the German Hospital, with two severe knife wounds. He told me he had received them from one of the assassins . . ."

"A man named Harding," Hall interrupted and guessed. "It happened up on the Nevada desert, near Winnemucca, on a railroad train."

"Yes, yes; that is the name. That is what he said."

"You see how everything dovetails," Hall urged. "There may be a great deal of madness in it, but the madness even is real, and you and I, at any rate, are sane."

"Yes, but let me hurry on." She pressed his arm with renewed confidence. "Oh, we have so much to tell each other. Uncle swears by you. But that is not what I want to say. I rented a furnished house, on the tip-top of Rincon Hill, and as soon as the doctors permitted, I moved Uncle Sergius to it. We've been keeping house there for the last few weeks. Uncle is entirely recovered—or Father, rather. He *is* my father. I believe that now, for it seems I must believe everything. And I shall believe . . . unless I wake up and find it all a nightmare. Now Un—Father has been tinkering about the house the last few days. Today, with everything packed for our voyage to Honolulu, he sent the luggage aboard the steamer, and sent me to a hotel. Now I know nothing about explosives, save glints and glimmerings from my reading; but just the same I know he has mined the house. He has dug up the cellar. He has opened the walls of the big living room and closed them again. I know he has run wires behind the partitions, and I know that today he was making things ready to run a wire from the house to a clump of shrubbery in the grounds near the gateway. Possibly you may guess what he plans to do."

Hall was just remembering John Gray's failure to keep the theatre engagement.

"Something is to happen there tonight," Grunya went on. "Uncle intends to join me later tonight at the St. Francis, or tomorrow morning on the steamer. In the meantime—"

But Hall, having reasoned his way to action, was urging her by the arm, back out of the park to the corner where stood the waiting row of taxicabs.

"In the meantime," he told her, "we must rush to Rincon Hill. He is going to kill them. We must prevent it."

"If only he isn't killed," she murmured. "The cowards! The cowards!"

"Pardon me, dear, but they are not cowards. They are brave men, and they are the most likable chaps, if a bit peculiar, under the sun. To know them is to love them. There has been too much killing already."

"They want to kill my father."

"And he wants to kill them," Hall retorted. "Don't forget that. And it is by his order. He is as mad as a hatter, and they are precisely as mad as so many more hatters. Come! Quick, please! Quick! They are assembling there now in the mined house. We may save them—or him, who knows?"

"Rincon Hill—time is money—you know what that means," he said to the taxi driver, as he helped Grunya in. "Come on, now! Burn up that juice! Rip up the pavement, anything you want, as long as you get us there!"

Rincon Hill, once the aristocratic residence district of San Francisco, lifts its head of decayed gentility from out of the muck and ruck of the great labor ghetto that spreads away south of Market Street. At the foot of the hill, Hall paid off the cab, and he and Grunya began the easy climb. Though it was still early in the evening, no more than half past nine, few persons were afoot. Chancing to glance back, Hall saw a familiar form pass across the circle of light shed by a street lamp. He drew Grunya into the house shadows of the side street and waited, and in a few minutes was rewarded by seeing Haas go by, walking in his peculiar, effortless, cat-like way. They continued on, half a block behind him, and when, at the crest of the hill, under the light from the next street lamp, they saw him vault a low, old-fashioned iron fence, Grunya nudged Hall's arm significantly.

"That is the house, our house," she whispered. "Watch him. Little he dreams he is going to his death."

"Little I dream he is either," Hall whispered back skeptically. "In my opinion Mr. Haas is a very difficult specimen to kill."

"Uncle Sergius is very careful. I have never known him to blunder. He has arranged everything, and when your Mr. Haas goes through that front door—"

She broke off. Hall had gripped her arm savagely.

"He's not going through that front door, Grunya. Watch him. He's prowling to the rear."

"There is no rear," she said. "The hill falls away in a bulkhead down to the next back yard, forty feet below. He'll prowl back to the front. The garden is very small."

"He's up to something," Hall muttered, as the dark form came in sight again. "Ah ha! Mr. Haas! You're the wily one! See, Grunya, he's crawled into that shrubbery by the gate. Is that where the wire was run?"

"Yes; it's the only thick clump of shrubbery a man can hide in. Here comes somebody. I wonder if it's another of the assassins."

Not waiting, Hall and Grunya walked on past the house to the next corner. The man who had come from the other direction turned into Dragomiloff's house and walked up the steps to the door. They heard it, after a momentary delay, open and shut.

Grunya insisted on accompanying Hall. It was her house, she said, and she knew every inch of it. Besides, she still had the pass-key, and it would not be necessary to ring.

The front hall was lighted, so that the house number showed plainly, and they walked boldly past the bushes that concealed Haas, unlocked the front door, and entered. Hall hung his hat on the rack and pulled off his gloves. From the door to the right came a murmur of voices. They paused outside to listen.

"Beauty *is* a compulsion," they heard one voice master the conversation.

"That's Hanover, the Boston associate," Hall whispered.

"Beauty is absolute," the voice went on. "Human life, all life, has been bent to beauty. It is not a case of paradoxical adaptation. Beauty was not bent to life. Beauty was in the universe when man was not. Beauty will remain in the universe when man has vanished and again is not. Beauty is—well, it is beauty, that is all, the first word and the last, and it does not depend upon little maggoty men a-crawl in the slime."

"Metaphysics," they could hear Lucoville sneer. "Pure illusory metaphysics, my dear Hanover. When a man begins to label as absolute the transient phenomena of an ephemeral evolution—"

"Metaphysician yourself," they heard Hanover interrupt. "You would contend that nothing exists save in consciousness, that when consciousness is destroyed, beauty is destroyed, that the thing itself, the vital principle to which developing life has been bent, is destroyed. When we know, all of us, and you should know it, that it is the principle only that persists. As Spencer has well said of the eternal flux of force and matter, with its alternate rhythm of evolution and dissolution, 'ever the same in principle but never the same in concrete result.' "

"New norms, new norms," Lucoville blurted in. "New norms ever appearing in successive and dissimilar evolutions."

"The norm itself!" Hanover cried triumphantly. "Have you considered that? You, yourself, have just asserted that the norm persists. What then, is the norm? It is the eternal, the absolute, the outside-of-consciousness, the father and the mother of consciousness."

"A moment," Lucoville cried excitedly.

"Bah!" Hanover went on with true scholarly dogmatism. "You attempt to resurrect the old exploded, Berkeleyan idealism. Metaphysics—generations behind the times. The modern school, as you ought to know, insists that the thing exists of itself. Consciousness, seeing and perceiving the thing, is a mere accident. 'Tis you, my dear Lucoville, who are the metaphysician."

There was a clapping of hands and rumble of approval.

"Hoist by your own petard," they heard one mellow voice cry in an unmistakable English accent.

"John Gray," Hall whispered to Grunya. "If the theatre were not so hopelessly commercialized, he would revolutionize the whole of it."

"Logomachy," they heard Lucoville begin his reply. "Word-mongering, tricks of speech, a shuffling of words and ideas. If you chaps will give me ten minutes, I'll expound my position."

"Behold!" Hall whispered. "Our amiable assassins, adorable philosophers. Now, would you rather believe them madmen than cruel and brutal murderers?"

Grunya shrugged her shoulders. "They may bend beauty any way they please, but I cannot forget that they are bent on killing Uncle Sergius—my father."

"But don't you see? They are obsessed by ideas. They take no count of mere human life—not even of their own. They are in slavery to thought. They live in a world of ideas."

"At fifty thousand per," she retorted.

It was his turn to shrug his shoulders.

"Come," he said. "Let us enter. No, I'll go first."

He turned the door handle and went in, followed by Grunya. The conversation stopped abruptly, and seven men, seated comfortably about the room, stared at the two intruders.

"Look here, Hall," Harkins said with evident irritation. "You were to be kept out of this. And we kept you out. Yet here you are, and with a—pardon me—a stranger."

"And if it had depended on you fellows, I should have been kept out," Hall answered. "Why so secret?"

"It was the Chief's orders. He invited us here. And since we obeyed his instructions and didn't let you in on it, our only conclusion is that it is he who let you in."

"No he didn't," Hall laughed. "And you might as well ask us to be seated. This, gentlemen, is Miss Constantine. Miss Constantine, Mr. Gray; Mr. Harkins; Mr. Lucoville; Mr. Breen; Mr. Alsworthy; Mr. Starkington; and Mr. Hanover—with the one exception of Mr. Haas, the surviving members of the Assassination Bureau."

"This is broken faith!" Lucoville cried angrily. "Hall, I am disappointed!"

"You do not understand, friend Lucoville. This is Miss Constantine's house. In the absence of her father you are her guests, all of you."

"We were given to understand it was Dragomiloff's house," Starkington said. "He told us so. We came separately; yet, since we all arrived here we can only conclude that there was no mistake of street and number."

"It is the same thing," Hall replied, with a quiet smile. "Miss Constantine is Dragomiloff's daughter."

On the instant Grunya and Hall were surrounded by the others, and hands were held out to her. Her own hand she put behind her, at the same time taking a backward step.

"You want to kill my father," she said to Lucoville. "It is impossible that I should take your hand."

"Here, this chair; be seated, dear lady," Lucoville was saying, assisted by Starkington and Gray in bringing the chair to her. "We are highly honored—the daughter of our Chief—we did not know he had a daughter—she is welcome—any daughter of our Chief is welcome—"

"But you want to kill him," she continued her objection. "You are murderers."

"We are friends, believe me. We represent an amity that is higher and deeper than life and death. Dear lady, human life is nothing—less than a bagatelle. Life! Why, our lives are mere pawns in the game of social evolution. We admire your father, we respect him; he is a great man. He is—or, rather, he was—our Chief."

"Yet you want to kill him," she persisted.

"And by his orders. Be seated, please." Lucoville succeeded in his attentions, insofar as she sank down in the chair. "This friend of yours, Mr. Hall," he went on. "You do not refuse him as a friend. You do not call him a murderer. Yet it was he who deposited the fifty-thousand-dollar fee for your father's life. You see, dear lady, already he has half destroyed our organization. Yet we do not hold it against him. He is our friend. We honor him because we know him to be a man, an honest man, a man of his word, an ethicist of no mean dimensions."

"Isn't it wonderful, Miss Constantine!" Hanover broke in ecstatically. "Amity that makes death cheap! The rule of right! The worship of right! Does it not make one hope? Think of it! It proves that the future is ours; that the future belongs to the right-thinking, right-acting man and woman; that such fierce, feeble stirrings and animal yearnings of the beastly clay, love of self and love of kindred flesh and blood, vanish away as dawn mist before the sun of the higher righteousness! Reason—and, mark me, *right reason*—triumphs! All the human world, some day, will comport itself, not according to the flesh and the abysmal mire, but according to high right reason!"

Grunya bowed her head and threw up her arms in admission of befuddled despair.

"You can't resist them, eh?" Hall exulted, bending over her.

"It is the chaos of super-thinking," she said helplessly. "It is ethics gone mad."

"So I told you," he answered. "They are all mad, as your

father is mad, as you and I are mad insofar as we are touched by their thinking. And now what do you think of our lovable assassins?"

"Yes, what do you think of us?" Hanover beamed over the top of his spectacles.

"All I can say," she replied, "is that you don't look like it—like assassins, I mean. As for you, Mr. Lucoville, I will take your hand, I will take the hands of all of you, if you will promise to give up this attempt to kill my father."

"You have a long way, Miss Constantine, to climb upwards to the light," Hanover chided regretfully.

"Kill? Kill?" Lucoville queried excitedly. "Why this fear of killing? Death is nothing. Only the beasts, the creatures of the mire, fear death. My dear lady, we are beyond death. We are full-statured intelligences, knowing good and evil. It is no more difficult for us to be killed than it is for us to kill. Killing—why, it occurs in every slaughterhouse and meat-canning establishment in the land. It is so common that it is almost vulgar."

"Who has not swatted a mosquito?" Starkington shouted. "With one fell swoop of a meat-nourished, death-nourished hand smashed to destruction a most wonderful, sentient, and dazzling flying mechanism? If there be tragedy in death—think of the mosquito, the squashed mosquito, the airy fairy miracle of flight disrupted and crushed as no aviator has ever been disrupted and crushed, not even MacDonald who fell fifteen thousand feet. Have you ever studied the mosquito, Miss Constantine? It will repay you. Why, the mosquito is just as wonderful, in the phenomena of living matter, as man is wonderful."

"But there *is* a difference," Gray put in.

"I was coming to that. And what is the difference? Swat the mosquito." He paused for emphasis. "Well, he is swatted, isn't he? And that is all. He is finished. The memory of him is not. But swat a man—by entire generations swat man—and something is left. What is it that is left? Not a peripatetic organism, not a hungry stomach, a bald head, and a mouthful of aching

teeth, but thoughts—royal, kingly thoughts. That's the difference. Thoughts! High thoughts! Right thoughts! Reasoned
righteousness!"

"Hold!" Hanover shouted, in his excitement springing to his
feet and waving his arms. "Swat—and I accept your word, Starkington, crude though it is, but expressive. Swat—and I warn you,
Starkington—swat as much as the tiniest pigment cell of the
diaphanous gauze of a new-hatched mosquito's wing, and the
totality of the universe is jarred from its central suns to the stars
beyond the stars. Do not forget there is a cosmic righteousness
in that pigment cell and in the last atom of the billion atoms that
go to compose that pigment cell, and in every one of the count-
less myriads of corpuscles that go to compose one of those billion
atoms."

"Listen, gentlemen," Grunya said. "What are you here for? I
do not mean in the universe, but here in this house. I accept all
that Mr. Hanover has so eloquently said of the pigment cell of
the mosquito's wing. It is evidently not right to—to swat a mosquito. Then, how in the name of sanity can you reconcile your
presence here, bent as you are on a red-handed murder, with the
ethics you have just expounded?"

An uproar of reconciliation arose from every mouth.

"Hey! Shut up!" Hall bellowed at them, then turned to the
girl and commanded peremptorily, "Grunya, stop it. You're getting touched. In five minutes you'll be as bad as they are. A truce
to argument, you fellows. Cut it out. Forget it. Let's get down
to business. Where is the Chief, Miss Constantine's father? You
say he told you to come here. Why have you come here? To
kill him?"

Hanover wiped his forehead, collapsed from his passion of
thought, and nodded.

"That is our reasoned intention," he said calmly. "Of course,
the presence of Miss Constantine is embarrassing. I fear we shall
have to ask her to withdraw."

"You are a brute, sir," she gravely assured the mild-mannered scholar. "I shall remain right here. And you won't kill my father. I tell you, you won't."

"Why isn't the Chief here, then?" Hall inquired.

"Because it is not yet time. He telephoned to us, talked with us himself, and he said he would meet us here in this room at ten o'clock. It is almost ten now."

"Maybe he won't come," Hall suggested.

"He gave his word," was the simple but quite convincing answer.

Hall looked at his watch. It marked a few seconds before ten. And ere those seconds had ticked off, the door opened and Dragomiloff, blond and colorless, clad in a gray traveling suit, stepped in, passing a glance over the assemblage from silken eyes of the palest blue.

"Greetings, dear friends and brothers," he said in his monotonously even voice. "I see you are all here, with the exception of Haas. Where is Haas?"

The assassins who could not lie stared at one another in awkward confusion.

"Where is Haas?" Dragomiloff repeated.

"We—ah—we don't know exactly, that is it, exactly," Harkins began haltingly.

"Well, I do, and exactly," Dragomiloff chopped him short. "I watched you arrive from the upstairs window. I recognized all of you. Haas also arrived. He is now lying in the shrubbery inside the gate on the right-hand side of the walk, and exactly four feet and four inches from the lower hinge of the gate. I measured it the other day. Do you think that was what I intended?"

"We did not care to anticipate your intentions, dear Chief," Hanover spoke up benignly, but with logical emphasis. "We debated your invitation and your instructions carefully, and it was our unanimous conclusion that we committed no breach of word or faith in assigning Haas to his position outside. Do you remember your instructions?"

"Perfectly," Dragomiloff assented. "Wait till I go over them to myself." For a half-minute of silence he reviewed his instructions, then his face thawed into almost a beam of satisfaction. "You are correct," he announced. "You have committed no breach of right conduct. And now, dear comrades, all our plans are destroyed by this intrusion of my daughter and of the man who is your Temporary Secretary and who I hope some day will be my son-in-law."

"What was the aim of your plan?" Starkington asked quickly.

"To destroy you," Dragomiloff laughed. "And the aim of your plan was?"

"To destroy you," Starkington admitted. "And destroy you we will. We regret Miss Constantine's presence, as we likewise do Mr. Hall's presence. They came uninvited. They can, of course, withdraw."

"I won't!" Grunya cried out. "You cold-blooded, inhuman, mathematical monsters! This is my father, and I may be abysmal mire, or anything else you please, but I will not withdraw, and you shall not harm him."

"You must meet me halfway in this," Dragomiloff urged. "Let us consider this once that we have failed on both sides. Let me propose a truce."

"Very well," Starkington conceded. "A truce for five minutes, during which time no overt act may be attempted and no one may leave the room. We should like to confer together over there by the piano. Is it agreed?"

"Yes, certainly. But first you will please notice where I am standing. My hand is resting against this particular book in this bookcase. I shall not move until you have decided on what course you intend to pursue."

The assassins drew to the far end of the room and began talking in whispers.

"Come," Grunya whispered to her father. "You have but to step through the door and escape."

Dragomiloff smiled forgivingly. "You do not understand," he said with gentleness.

She clenched her hands passionately, crying, "You are as insane as they."

"But Grunya, love," he pleaded, "is it not a beautiful insanity—if you prefer the misnomer? Here thought rules and right rules. It would seem to me the highest rationality and control. What distinguishes man from the lower animals is control. Witness this scene. There stand seven men intent on killing me. Here I stand intent on killing them. Yet, by the miracle of the spoken word we agree to a truce. We trust. It is a beautiful example of high moral inhibition."

"Every hermit, on top of a pillar or living with the snakes in a cliff cave, has been a beautiful example of such inhibition," she came back impatiently. "The inhibitions practiced in the asylums are often very remarkable."

But Dragomiloff refused to be drawn, and smiled and joked until the assassins returned. As before, Starkington was the spokesman.

"We have decided," he said, "that it is our duty to kill you, dear Chief. There is still a minute to run. When it is gone we shall proceed to our work. Also, in that interval, we again request our two unbidden guests to withdraw."

Grunya shook her head positively. "I am armed," she threatened, drawing a small automatic pistol and displaying her inexperience by not pressing down the safety catch.

"It's too bad," Starkington apologized. "But we shall have to go on with our work just the same."

"If nothing unforeseen prevents?" Dragomiloff suggested.

Starkington glanced at his comrades, who nodded, then said, "Certainly, unless nothing unforeseen—"

"And here is the unforeseen," Dragomiloff interrupted quietly. "You see my hands, my dear Starkington. They bear no weapons. Forbear a minute. You see the book against which my left hand rests. Behind that book, at the back of the case, is a push-button. One firm thrust in of the book presses the button. The room is a magazine of dynamite. Need I explain more? Draw aside that rug on which you are standing—that's right. Now carefully lift up that loose board. See the sticks lying side by side. They're all connected."

"Most interesting," Hanover murmured, peering down at the dynamite through his spectacles. "Death so simply achieved! A violent chemical reaction, I believe. Some day, when I can spare the time, I shall make a study of explosives."

And in that moment, Hall and Grunya realized that the philosopher-assassins were truly not afraid of death. As they claimed for themselves, they were not burdened by the flesh. Love of life did not yearn through their mental processes. All they knew was the love of thought.

"We did not guess this," Gray assured Dragomiloff. "But we apprehended what we did not guess. That is why we stationed Haas outside. You could escape us, but not him."

"Which reminds me, comrades," Dragomiloff said. "I ran another wire to the spot in the grounds where Haas is now lurking. Let us hope he does not blunder upon my button I concealed there, else we'll all go up along with our theories. Suppose one of you goes and brings him in to join us. And while we're about it, let us agree to another truce. Under the present circumstances, your hands are tied."

"Seven lives for one," said Harkins. "Mathematically it is repulsive."

"It is poor economics," Breen agreed.

"And suppose," Dragomiloff continued, "we make the truce till one o'clock and you all come and have supper with me."

"If Haas agrees," Alsworthy said. "I am going to get him now."

Haas agreed and, like any party of friends, they left the house together and caught an electric car for uptown.

13

In a private room at the Poodle Dog, the eight assassins and Dragomiloff, Hall, and Grunya sat at table. And a merry, almost convivial supper it was, despite the fact that Harkins and Hanover were vegetarians, that Lucoville eschewed all cooked food and munched bovinely at a great plate of lettuce, raw turnips, and carrots, and that Alsworthy began, kept up, and finished with nuts, raisins, and bananas. On the other hand, Breen, who looked a dyspeptic, orgied with a thick, raw steak and shuddered at the suggestion of wine. Dragomiloff and Haas drank thin native claret, while Hall, Gray, and Grunya shared a pint of light Rhine wine. Starkington, however, began with two Martini cocktails, and ever and again, throughout the meal, buried his face in a huge stein of Würzburger.

The talk was outspoken, though the feeling displayed was comradely and affectionate.

"We'd have got you," Starkington told Dragomiloff, "if it hadn't been for the inopportune arrival of your daughter."

"My dear Starkington," Dragomiloff retorted. "It was she who saved you. I'd have bagged the seven of you."

"No you wouldn't," Breen joined in. "As I understand, the wire led to the bushes where Haas was hiding."

"His being there was an accident, a mere accident," Dragomiloff answered lightly enough, yet unable to conceal that he was somewhat crestfallen.

"Since when has the fortuitous been discarded from the factors of evolution?" Hanover began learnedly.

"You'd never have touched it off, Chief," Haas was saying at the same time that Lucoville was demanding of Hanover, "Since when was the fortuitous ever classed as a factor?"

"Possibly your disagreement is merely of definition," Hall said pacifically. "That asparagus is tinned, Hanover. Did you know that?"

Hanover forgot the argument, and sat back aghast. "And I never eat tinned stuff of any sort! Are you sure, Hall? Are you sure?"

"Ask the waiter. He'll tell you the same."

"It's all right, dear Haas," Dragomiloff was saying. "The next time I'll surely touch it off, and you won't be in the way. You'll be at the other end of the wire."

"Oh, I cannot understand, I cannot understand," Grunya cried. "It seems a joke. It can't be real. Here you are, all good friends, eating and drinking together and affectionately telling how you intend killing one another." She turned to Hall. "Wake me up, Winter. This is a dream."

"I wish it were."

She turned to Dragomiloff. "Oh, Uncle Sergius, wake me up!"

"You are awake, Grunya, love."

"Then if I'm awake," she went on, firmly, almost angrily, "it is you who are the somnambulists. Wake up! Oh, wake up! I wish an earthquake would come, anything, if it would only rouse you. Father, you can do it. Withdraw that order for your death which you yourself gave."

"But don't you see, he can't," Starkington told her across the corner of the table.

Dragomiloff, at the other end of the table, shook his head. "You would not have me break my word, Grunya?"

"I'm not afraid to break—anything!" Hall interrupted. "The order started with me. I withdraw it. Return my fifty thousand, or spend it on charity. I don't care. The point is, I don't want Dragomiloff killed."

"You forget yourself," Haas reminded him. "You are merely

a client of the Bureau. And when you engaged the service of the Bureau, you agreed to certain things. The Bureau likewise agreed to certain things. You may wish to break your agreement, but it has passed beyond you. The affair is in the hands of the Bureau, and the Bureau does not break its agreements. It never has broken them and it never will. If there be not absolute faith in the given word, if the given word be not as unbreakable as the tie-ribs of earth, then there is no hope in life, and creation crashes to chaos because of its intrinsic falsity. We deny this falsity. We prove it by our acts that clinch the finality of the given word. Am I right, comrades?"

Approval was unanimous, and Dragomiloff, half rising from his chair, reached across and grasped the hand of Haas. For once Dragomiloff's undeviating, monotonous voice was touched with the emphasis of feeling as he proclaimed proudly:

"The hope of the world! The higher race! The top of evolution! The right-rulers and king-thinkers! The realization of all dreams and aspirings; the slime crawled upward to the light; the touch and the promise of Godhead come true!"

Hanover left his seat and threw his arms about the Chief in an ecstasy of intellectual admiration and fellowship. Grunya and Hall looked at each other despairingly.

"King-thinkers," he murmured helplessly.

"The asylums are filled with king-thinkers," was her angry comment.

"Logic!" he sneered.

"I, too, shall write a book," she added. "It shall be entitled *The Logic of Lunacy, or, Why Thinkers Go Mad*."

"Never has our logic been better vindicated," Starkington said to her, as the jubilation of the king-thinkers eased down.

"You do violence with your logic," Grunya flung back. "I will prove it to you—"

"By logic?" Gray interpolated quickly and raised a general laugh, in which Grunya could not help but join.

Hall lifted his hand solemnly for a hearing.

"We have yet to debate how many angels can dance on the point of a needle."

"Shame on you!" Lucoville cried. "That is antediluvian. We are scholars, not scholastics——"

"And you can prove it," Grunya stabbed across, "as easily as you can the angels and the needle and everything else."

"If ever I get out of this mix-up with you fellows," Hall declared, "I shall forswear logic. Never again!"

"A confession of intellectual fatigue," Lucoville argued.

"Only he does not mean it," Harkins put in. "He can't help being logical. It is his heritage—the heritage of man. It distinguishes man from the lesser——"

"Hold!" Hanover broke in. "You forget that the universe is founded on logic. Without logic the universe could not be. In every fibre of it logic resides. There is logic in the molecule, in the atom, in the electron. I have a monograph, here in my pocket, which I shall read to you. I have called it 'Electronic Logic.' It——"

"Here is the waiter," Hall interrupted wickedly. "He says of course that the asparagus was tinned."

Hanover ceased fumbling in his pocket in order to vent a tirade against the waiter and the management of the Poodle Dog.

"That was not logical," Hall smiled, when the waiter had left the room.

"And why not, pray?" Hanover asked, with a touch of asperity.

"Because it is not the season for fresh asparagus."

Ere Hanover could recover from this, Breen began on him.

"You said earlier this evening, Hanover, that you were interested in explosives. Let me show you the quintessence of universal logic—the irrefragable logic of the elements, the logic of chemistry, the logic of mechanics, and the logic of time, all indissolubly welded together into one of the prettiest devices ever mortal mind conceived. So thoroughly do I agree with you, that I shall now show you the unreasoned logic of the stuff of the universe."

"Why unreasoned?" Hanover queried faintly, shuddering at the uneaten asparagus. "Do you think the electron incapable of reason?"

"I don't know. I never saw an electron. But for the sake of the argument, let us suppose it does reason. Anyway, as you'll agree, it's the keenest logic, the absolutest and most unswervable logic you've ever seen. Look at that." Breen had gone to where his overcoat hung on the wall and drawn out a flat oblong package. This, when unwrapped, resembled a folding pocket camera of medium size. He held it up with eyes sparkling with admiration. "By George, Hanover!" he exclaimed. "I think you are right. Look at it!—The eloquent-voiced, the subduer of jarring tongues and warring creeds, the ultimate arbiter. It enunciates the final word. When it speaks, kings and emperors, grafters and falsifiers, the Scribes and Pharisees and all wrong-thinkers remain silent—forever remain silent."

"Let it speak," Haas grinned. "Maybe it will silence Hanover."

The laughter died away as they saw Breen, the object poised in his hand, visibly thinking. And in the silence they saw him achieve his concept of action.

"Very well," he said. "It shall speak." He drew from his vest pocket an ordinary-looking, gun-metal watch. "It is an alarm watch," he went on, "seventeen-jeweled movement, Swiss-Elgin works. Let me see. It is now midnight. Our truce"—he bowed to Dragomiloff—"expires at one o'clock. See, I set it for precisely one minute after one." He pointed to an opening in the camera-like object. "Behold this slot. It is specially devised to receive this watch—mark me, I say, specially devised. I insert the watch, thus. Did you hear that metallic click? That is the automatic locking device. No power can now remove that watch. I cannot. The decree has gone forth. It cannot be recalled. All this is of my devising save for the voice itself. The voice is the voice of Nakatodaka, the great Japanese who died last year."

"A phonograph record," Hanover complained. "I thought you said something about explosives."

"The voice of Nakatodaka is an explosive," Breen expounded. "Nakatodaka, if you will remember, was killed in his laboratory by his own voice."

"Formose!" Haas said, nodding his head. "I remember now."

"So do I," Hall told Grunya. "Nakatodaka was a great chemist."

"But I understand the secret died with him," Starkington said.

"So the world understood," was Breen's reply. "But the formula was found by the Japanese government and stolen from the War Office by a revolutionist." His voice swelled with pride. "This is the first Formose ever manufactured on American soil. I manufactured it."

"Heavens!" Grunya cried. "And when it goes off it will blow us all up!"

Breen nodded with intense gratification.

"If you remain it will," he said. "The people in this neighborhood will think it an earthquake or another anarchist outrage."

"Stop it!" she commanded.

"I can't. That's the beauty of it. As I told Hanover, it is the logic of chemistry, the logic of mechanics, and the logic of time, all indissolubly welded together. There is no power in the universe that can now break that weld. Any attempt would merely precipitate the explosion."

Grunya caught Hall's hand as she stared at him in her helplessness, but Hanover, fluttering and hovering about the infernal machine, peering at it delightedly through his spectacles, was off in another ecstasy.

"Wonderful! Wonderful! Breen, I congratulate you. We shall now be able to settle the affairs of nations and put the world on a higher, nobler basis. Hebrew is a diversion. This is an efficiency. I shall certainly devote myself to the study of explosives . . . Lucoville, you are refuted. There *is* morality in the elements, and reason, and logic.''

"You forget, my dear Hanover," Lucoville replied, "that behind this mechanism and chemistry and abstraction of time is the mind of man, devising, controlling, utilizing——"

But he was interrupted by Hall, who had shoved his chair back and sprung to his feet.

"You lunatics! You sit there like a lot of clams! Don't you realize that that damned thing is going to go off?"

"Not until one after one," Hanover mildly assured him. "Besides, Breen has not yet told us his intentions."

"The mind of man behind and informing unconscious matter and blind force," Lucoville gibed.

Starkington leaned across to Hall and said in an undertone, "Transport this scene to a stage setting with a Wall Street audience! There'd be a panic."

But Hall shook the interruption aside.

"Look here, Breen, just what is your intention? I, for one, and Miss Constantine, are going to get out, now, at once."

"There is plenty of time," replied the custodian of Nakatodaka's voice. "I'll tell you my intention. The truce expires at one. I am between our dear Chief and the door. He can't go through the walls. I guard the door. The rest of you may depart. But I remain here with him. The blow is sped. Nothing can stop it. One minute after the truce is up the last commission accepted by the Bureau will have been accomplished. Pardon me, dear Chief, one moment. I have told you that even I cannot stop the process now at work in that mechanism. But I can expedite it. You see my thumb, lightly resting in this depression? It just barely brushes a button. One press of the thumb, and the machine immediately explodes. Now, as an honorable and logical man and comrade, you can see that any attempt of yours to get out of this door will blow all of us up, your daughter and the Temporary Secretary as well. Therefore you will remain in your seat. Hanover, the formula is safe. I shall remain here and die with the Chief at one minute after one. You will find the formula in the top drawer of the filing cabinet in my bedroom."

"Do something!" Grunya entreated Hall. "You must do something."

Hall, who had sat down, again stood up, moving the wineglass to one side as he rested one hand on the table.

"Gentlemen." He spoke in a quiet voice, but one which immediately gained him the respectful attention of the others. "Until now, despite my abhorrence of killing, I have felt bound to respect the ideals that directed your actions. Now, however, I must question your motives."

He turned to Breen, who was watching him carefully.

"Tell me," Hall pursued, "do you feel that you, personally, merit extinction? If you give your life in order to assassinate your Chief, you are violating the tenet that any death at your hand is one warranted by the crimes of the victim. Of what crimes are you so guilty as to make this sentence—which you have passed upon yourself—a just one?"

Breen smiled at this adroit argument. The others listened politely.

"But you see," the bacteriologist explained happily, "we in the Assassination Bureau recognize the possibility of our own death in the execution of our assignments. It is a normal risk of our business."

"Accidental death, yes, as a result of the unexpected," was Hall's quiet reply. "Here, however, we are speaking of a planned death, and that of an innocent person—yourself. This is in violation of your own principles."

There was a moment's thoughtful silence.

"He's quite right, Breen, you know," Gray finally offered. He had been listening to the verbal duel with puckered forehead. "I'm afraid that your solution is scarcely acceptable."

"Still," Lucoville contributed, "consider this: Breen, by arranging an innocent's death, might be warranting his own death for dereliction of principle."

"A priori," Haas snapped impatiently. "Specious. You are arguing in circles. Until he dies, he is not guilty; if he is not guilty, he does not warrant death."

"Mad!" Grunya whispered. "They are all mad!"

She stared at the animated faces about the festive table with awe. They had the intent gleam in their eyes of scholars at a seminar. No one seemed in the slightest affected by the knowledge of the deadly bomb ticking away the minutes. Breen had released his thumb from the small button on the side of the weapon. His eyes followed each speaker eagerly as they argued his proposal.

"There is one possible solution," Harkins remarked slowly, leaning forward to join the discussion. "Breen, by setting the bomb during the period of a truce, was dishonoring a commitment. I do not say that this, of itself, merits a punishment as severe as he contemplates, but certainly he has been guilty of an action beyond the strict morality of our organization . . ."

"True!" cried Breen, his eyes sparkling. "It is true, and that is the answer! By speeding the blow during an armistice, I have committed a sin. I find myself guilty and deserving of death." His eyes flashed to the wall-clock. "In exactly thirty minutes . . ."

But his inattention to Dragomiloff proved fatal. Swift as a striking cobra, the strong hands of the ex-Chief of the Bureau sought and found vital nerves in Breen's neck. The death-touch of the Japanese was immediately effective; even as the others watched in startled surprise Breen's hand relaxed on the small bomb and he slid lifeless to the floor. In almost the same motion Dragomiloff had snatched up his coat and was at the door.

"I shall see you on the boat, Grunya, my dear," he murmured, and was through and away before any of the others could move.

"After him!" cried Harkins, springing to his feet. But he found his way barred by the tall form of John Gray.

"There is a truce!" Gray reminded him fiercely. "Breen broke it and has paid dearly for his dereliction. We are still bound by our honor for another twenty minutes."

Starkington, who had watched the entire discussion dispassionately from one end of the long table, lifted his head and spoke.

"The bomb," he observed quietly. "Our polemics, I am afraid, will have to be postponed. There are exactly—" he glanced at the wall-clock "—eighteen minutes until it is scheduled to detonate."

Haas leaned down curiously, picking the small box from Breen's lax hand.

"There must be a way . . ."

"Breen assured us there was not," Starkington responded dryly. "I believe him. Breen never equivocated in a scientific statement." He came to his feet. "As head of the Chicago office I must assume command of our greatly reduced forces. Harkins, you and Alsworthy must take the bomb to the Bay as quickly as possible. We cannot leave it here to explode and kill innocents."

He waited as the two men took their coats and left, carrying the deadly ticking container of Formose.

"Our respected ex-Chief made mention of a boat," he continued evenly. "I had assumed this was his motive in coming to San Francisco; his statement merely confirmed it. Since we cannot stoop to extracting the name of the steamer from his lovely daughter, we must make other arrangements. Haas . . . ?"

"There are but three steamers sailing in the morning with the tide," responded Haas almost mechanically, while Grunya marveled at the wealth of information stored behind the bulging brow. "There are enough of us remaining to check easily upon all of them."

"Good," Starkington agreed. "They are . . . ?"

"The *Argosy*, at Oakland; the *Eastern Clipper* at Jansen's Wharf, and the *Takku Maru* at the Commercial Dock."

"Fine. Then Lucoville, you will take the *Argosy*. Haas, the

Takku Maru should be more suitable for you. Gray, the *Eastern Clipper*."

The three men rose alertly, but Starkington waved them to their seats.

"There is time until the tide, gentlemen," he remarked easily. "Besides, there are still twelve minutes remaining of our armistice." He stared at the body of Breen lying twisted on the floor. "We must make arrangements for the removal of our dear friend here, as well. An unfortunate heart attack, I should say. Hanover, if you would handle the telephone . . . Thank you."

His hand reached over to the table to find a wine-list.

"After which I would suggest a brandy, a bodied brandy. Possibly from Spain. A fitting drink, taken at the end of a repast. We shall drink, gentlemen, to the end of a most difficult assignment. And we shall toast, gentlemen, the man who made the assignment possible."

Hall swung about to object to this macabre humor at his expense, but before he could speak, the even voice of Starkington continued quietly.

"We shall toast, gentlemen: Ivan Dragomiloff!"

14

Winter Hall, aided by a full purse, experienced little difficulty in convincing the purser that space was available, even for a late-comer, aboard the *Eastern Clipper*. He had stopped briefly at his hotel for a bag, had left a short note to be delivered first thing in the morning, and had met an anxious Grunya at the gang-plank. While he was completing his financial arrangements for passage, Grunya disappeared below to inform her father of Hall's presence aboard ship. An elfin smile lit Dragomiloff's features.

"Did you expect me to be angry, my dear?" he inquired. "Upset? Or even surprised? While the thought of a trip alone with my newly discovered daughter is enjoyable, it will be even more enjoyable to travel with her when she is happy."

"You have always made me happy, Uncle—I mean, Father," she pouted, but her eyes were twinkling.

Dragomiloff laughed.

"There comes a time, my dear, when a father is limited in the happiness he can impart. And now, if you do not mind, I shall sleep. It has been a tiring day."

Grunya kissed him tenderly and was opening the door when memory struck.

"Father," she exclaimed. "The Assassination Bureau! They intend to investigate every ship sailing on the morning's tide."

"But of course," he said gently. "It is the first thing they would do." He kissed her again and closed the door behind her.

She mounted to the upper deck and found Hall. Hand in hand they stood at the rail, peering at the lights of the sleeping city. His hand tightened on hers.

"Must it really be a year?" he asked sadly.

"There are only three months remaining," she laughed. "Do not be impatient." Her laughter faded. "In truth, this is advice more suitable to myself."

"Grunya!"

"It is true," she admitted. "Oh, Winter, I want to be married to you so much!"

"Darling! The captain of the ship can marry us tomorrow!"

"No. I am as mad as all of you. I have given my word and I will not change it." She faced him soberly. "Until the year is up I will not marry you. And should anything happen to my father before then . . ."

"Nothing will happen to him," Hall assured her.

She looked at him steadily.

"Yet you will not promise me to prevent anything from happening."

"My darling, I cannot." Hall stared over the rail at the darkened waters below. "These madmen—and I must include your father in that category—will not allow anyone to interfere in their dangerous game. And that's what it is to them, you know. A game."

"Which no one can win," she agreed sadly, and then glanced at her time-piece. "It is very late. I really must go to sleep. Shall I see you in the morning?"

"You can scarcely avoid me on a small steamer," he laughed, and bending his head he kissed her fingers passionately.

Dragomiloff, finding his cabin warm, unbolted the porthole and swung it wide. His stateroom fronted upon the dockside and a solid row of inscrutable warehouses lit only by a row of small electric bulbs, swinging faintly in the night breeze. The maneuver resulted in little improvement; the night without was sultry and quiet.

He stood in the dark of his room, leaning against the brass rim of the porthole, breathing deeply. His thoughts ranged over the past nine months and the narrow escapes he had managed. He felt tired, mentally and physically tired. Age, he thought. The one variable in life's equation beyond the power of the brain to control or to evaluate. At least there were ten days ahead of freedom from stress; ten pleasant days of sea-voyage in which to recuperate. Suddenly, as he stood there, he heard a familiar voice rising from the shadows below.

"You are certain? Dragomiloff. It is very possible that he is a passenger aboard."

"Quite sure," the purser replied. "There is no one of that name on the ship. You may be certain that we would do everything in our power to aid the Federal government."

In the safety of his darkened stateroom, Dragomiloff grinned. His weariness fled as, all senses alert, he listened intently. Gray was clever to adopt the guise of a Federal man, but then Gray had always been extremely worthy of his position in the Bureau.

"There is a chance this man is not using his real name," Gray pursued. "He is a smallish person, deceptively frail-looking—although, believe me, he is not—and he is traveling with his daughter, a quite beautiful young lady whose name is Grunya."

"There is a gentleman traveling with his daughter . . ."

Dragomiloff's smile deepened. In the blackness of his room his small, strong fingers flexed and unflexed themselves preparatorily.

There was a moment's silence on the dock below; then Gray spoke thoughtfully.

"I should like to check further if you don't mind. Could you give me his cabin number?"

"Of course. One second, sir. Here it is—31—on the lower deck." There was a hesitant pause. "But if you should be wrong . . ."

"I shall apologize." There was coldness in Gray's voice. "The Federal government has no interest in embarrassing innocent people. But still, I have my duty to perform."

The shadowy figures at the foot of the gangplank separated,

the taller one mounting the inclined stairway easily, brushing past the other.

"I can find it, thank you. There is no need for you to leave your post."

"Certainly, sir. I hope . . ."

But Gray was beyond earshot. Stepping lightly to the deck of the ship he strode quickly to a door leading to an inner passageway. Once inside he immediately checked the numbers on the cabins facing him. The door before him was marked 108; without hesitation he swung to the stairway and descended. Here the numbers were of two digits. He smiled to himself and crept along the silent corridor, marking each door.

Number 31 lay beyond a turn in the passage, set in a small alcove. Flattening himself against the wall of the alcove, Gray considered his next step. He did not underestimate Dragomiloff, who had taught him not only the beauty of logic, ethics, and morality, but who had also taught him to break a man's neck with one swift blow. There was a sudden shudder to the ship, and he stiffened, but it was only the great engines below beginning to revolve, warming up preparatory to sailing.

In the silence of the deserted corridor Gray considered and rejected the thought of using his revolver. In the confined space the sound would be deafening, escape made that much more difficult. Instead he withdrew a thin, sharp knife from a holster on his forearm, and tested the edge briefly against his thumb. Satisfied, he gripped it firmly, edge uppermost, while his other hand crept to the lock, master-key in hand.

One quick glance assured him that he was alone in the passageway; the passengers were all asleep. As silently as possible he inserted the key, turning it slowly.

To his surprise the door was suddenly jerked inwards. Before he could recover his balance he was being pulled into the room and strong fingers were being clamped upon the hand holding the knife. But Gray's reactions had always been swift. Rather than pulling back, he went forward with his assailant, pushing fiercely, adding his weight to the impetus of the other's force. The two men fell in a sprawl against the bunk beneath the porthole. With a sudden heave, Gray was on his feet, twisting to one side, the knife once more firmly in position in his fingers. Dragomiloff was also on his feet, hands outstretched, his taut fingers searching for an opening to give a death-touch to his opponent.

For a moment they stood panting a few feet from one another. The small electric lights from the dock gave the cabin eerie shadows. Then, swift as lightning, Gray's arm flashed forwards, the knife whistling in the darkness. But it encountered only empty air; Dragomiloff had dropped to the floor, and as the other's arm swept above him he reached up and clutched it, twisting. With a smothered cry Gray dropped the knife and fell upon the smaller man, straining with his free hand for a grip on the other's throat.

They fought in fury and in silence, two trained assassins each aware of the other's ability and each convinced of the rightness, as well as the necessity, for the other's death. Each hold and counter-hold was automatic; their proficiency in the death-science of the Japanese equal and devastating. Beneath them the rumble of the huge pistons slowly turning over increased. Within the stateroom the battle waged relentlessly, grip matching grip, their panting breath now lost in the larger sound of the ship's engines.

Their thrashing legs encountered the open door; it slammed shut. Gray attempted to roll free and suddenly felt his lost knife pressing against his shoulder blades. With a thrust of his arched back he rolled further, fending off Dragomiloff's attack with one hand while he searched for the weapon with his other. And then his fingers found it. Twisting violently, he pulled free, swinging the blade for a frontal blow, and thrust it forward viciously. He felt it bite into something soft and for one second he relaxed. And in that moment Dragomiloff's eager fingers found the spot they had been seeking. Gray fell back, his fingers dragging the knife from the mattress of the bunk with their last dying effort.

Dragomiloff staggered to his feet, staring sombrely down at

the shadowy figure of his old friend lying at the foot of the narrow bunk. He leaned against the closed porthole, fighting to regain his breath, aware of how much the years had taken from his fighting ability. He rubbed his face wearily. Still, he thought, he had not succumbed to Gray's attack, and Gray was as deadly as any member.

A sudden rap at the door brought immediate awareness to him. He bent swiftly, rolling the dead body out of sight beneath the bunk, and came quietly to stand beside the door.

"Yes?"

"Mr. Constantine? Could I see you a moment, sir?"

"One second."

Dragomiloff switched on the stateroom light; a swift glance about the room revealed nothing too incriminating. He straightened a chair, threw the blanket back to conceal the torn mattress, and slipped into a dressing-gown. He glanced about once more. Satisfied that all was presentable, he opened the door a crack and yawned widely into the face of the purser.

"Yes? What is it?"

The purser looked embarrassed.

"A Mr. Gray, sir. Did he stop down to see you?"

"Oh, that. Yes, he did. But it was really too bad his bothering me, you know. He was looking for a Mr. Dragomovitch, or something. He apologized and left. Why?"

"The ship is sailing, sir. Do you suppose he might have gone ashore in the last few moments? While I was coming down here?"

Dragomiloff yawned again and stared at the purser coldly.

"I'm sure I have no idea. And now, if you'll excuse me, I really would like to get some rest."

"Certainly, sir. I'm sorry. Thank you."

Dragomiloff locked the door and once again switched off the lights. He sat on the small chair furnished with the stateroom and stared at the locked porthole thoughtfully. Tomorrow would be too late; there would be stewards cleaning the cabins. Even morning would be too late; early strollers about the decks were not uncommon. It would have to be now, with all the attendant dangers. With patience he settled back to await the ship's departure.

Voices came from the deck above as lines were cast off and the ship prepared to leave the dock. The rumble of the engines increased; a slight motion was imparted to the cabin. Above his head the faint pounding of feet could be heard as seamen ran back and forth, winching in the lines, obeying the exigencies of the steel monster which was to take them across the ocean.

The cries on deck abated. Dragomiloff carefully unbolted the porthole and thrust his head out. The watery gap between the pier and the ship was slowly widening; the lights strung along the warehouses were fading in the distance. He listened carefully for footsteps from above; there were none. Returning to his task he rolled the body free from its hiding place and, bending, lifted it with ease to prop it on the bunk. One last searching glance indicated that the coast was clear. He thrust the flaccid arms through the porthole and fed the body into the open air. It fell with a faint splash; Dragomiloff waited quietly for any outbreak of sound from above. There was none. With graven face he latched the porthole, pulled the drapes tightly over them, and re-lit the light.

One final check was necessary before retiring, for Dragomiloff was a thorough man. The knife was stowed in a suitcase, and the bag locked. The slit in the mattress was covered with the sheet, reversed and tucked in tightly. The rug was straightened. Only when the room had regained its former appearance did Dragomiloff relax and slowly begin undressing.

It had been a busy night, but one step further along his inexorable path.

15

Lucoville rapped sharply upon Starkington's hotel-room door and when the door swung back, entered and quietly laid a newspaper upon the table. Starkington's eye immediately caught the black headlines, and he read through the lurid account rapidly.

TWO DIE IN MYSTERIOUS EXPLOSION

Aug. 15: A mysterious explosion in the early hours of today on Worth Street near the Bay region caused the tragic death of two unidentified men. Police could discover no clue as to the cause of the violent detonation, which broke windows in the immediate vicinity, as well as costing the lives of the two men who were believed to be walking in the area at the time of the explosion.

The violence of the detonation made identification of the two victims impossible. The shattered fragments of a small metal box were the only unusual item found in the area, but police claim it could not possibly have played a part in the tragedy because of its size. At present the authorities admit themselves baffled.

"Harkins and Alsworthy!" he exclaimed through clenched teeth. "We must get the others here as quickly as possible!"

"I have telephoned to Haas and Hanover," Lucoville replied. "They should be here at any moment."

"And Gray?"

"His hotel room did not answer. I am rather surprised, since it was agreed that a report be made this morning on the ships that were investigated last night."

"You found nothing at the *Argosy*?"

"Nothing. Nor did Haas at the *Takku Maru*."

The two men stared at each other in silent common thought.

"Do you suppose . . . ?" Starkington began, but at that moment there was an imperious rap at the door, and before either occupant could answer, the door swung wide, revealing Hanover and Haas.

Haas rushed in, laying a later edition of the newspaper upon the table.

"Did you see this?" he cried. "Gray is dead!"

"Dead?"

"Found floating alongside Jansen's Wharf, where the *Eastern Clipper* was docked! Dragomiloff is on that ship, and it has sailed!"

There was a moment's shocked silence. Starkington walked over and slowly seated himself. His eyes roved the stern faces of his companions before he spoke.

"Well, gentlemen," he said softly, "we are being decimated. The total remaining members of the Assassination Bureau are within this room at this moment. Three of our number died within the past twelve hours. Where is the success that crowned our every effort for all these years? Can it all have departed at the same moment?"

"There are limits to one's infallibility," Haas objected. "Harkins and Alsworthy died as the result of an accident."

"Accident? You do not honestly believe that, Haas. You cannot. There is no such thing as an accident. We control our own lives, or we control nothing."

"Or at least we believe that, or we believe nothing," Lucoville amended dryly.

"But the wall-clock must have been wrong!" Haas insisted.

"Obviously," Starkington admitted. "But is it an accident to fail through dependence upon a mechanical contrivance? Inventions, my dear Haas, are the work of doers, and not thinkers."

"A ridiculous statement," Haas sneered.

"Not at all. It is the inability mentally to rationalize problems that leads men to seek mechanical solutions. Take that wall-clock, for example. Does the knowledge of the exact hour solve the problems of that hour? What is gained, in beauty or morality, to know that at this moment it is eight minutes past the hour of ten?"

"You oversimplify," Haas retorted. "Someday the clock may take its revenge."

Hanover leaned forwards.

"As for your sneering at doers," he remarked, "do you consider us, then, as only thinkers and not doers?"

Starkington smiled.

"Of late, to be truthful, we have been neither. Now we must be both."

Lucoville, who had been standing at a window staring into the street, swung about.

"Look here," he said flatly. "Dragomiloff has sailed. He has left the country. It is doubtful that he will return. Why do we not give up this senseless chase? We can rebuild the Bureau ourselves. Dragomiloff began it with one—himself—and we are four."

"Give up the chase?" Haas was shocked. "Senseless? How could we rebuild the Bureau if the first thing we give up is not the chase, but our principles?"

Lucoville bowed his head.

"You are right, of course. I was not thinking. Well, then, what is our next step?"

Haas answered him. The thin flame of a man arose and bent over the table, his huge forehead puckered.

"There is a ship sailing at four this afternoon—the *Oriental Star*—from Dearborn Slip. It is the fastest ship on the Pacific run.

It should easily dock in Hawaii a day in advance of the *Eastern Clipper's* arrival. I suggest that we be waiting for Dragomiloff when he arrives in Honolulu. And that we be more careful than our predecessors when we meet him."

"It is an excellent idea," Hanover agreed enthusiastically. "He will feel himself safe."

"The Chief never feels himself safe," Starkington commented. "It is only that he does not allow his feeling of un-safety to disturb him. Well, gentlemen; does Haas's suggestion sit well with you?"

There was a moment's silence. Then Lucoville shook his head.

"I do not believe it necessary that we all travel. Haas has still not recovered fully from his wound. Also, I do not believe it well to put all our eggs in one basket. I suggest that Haas remain. There may well be need for some action from the mainland."

This suggestion was carefully considered by the other three. Starkington nodded.

"I agree. Haas?"

The small intense man smiled ruefully.

"I should, of course, enjoy being in at the kill. But I must bow to the logic of Lucoville's argument. I also agree."

Hanover nodded his acceptance.

"We have sufficient funds?"

Starkington reached over and extracted an envelope from his desk.

"This was delivered by messenger this morning. Hall has signed a paper giving me power of withdrawal of our funds."

Hanover raised his eyebrows.

"He has traveled with Dragomiloff, then."

"With the daughter, rather," Haas corrected with a smile. "Poor Hall! Trapped by love into acquiring a father-in-law he has paid to have killed!"

"Hall's logic is tainted by emotion," Starkington commented. "The fate of the emotional is not only predictable, but usually deserved." He arose. "Well, then, I shall arrange for our passage." He stared at Lucoville in sudden concern. "Why do you frown?"

"The food aboard ship," Lucoville sighed unhappily. "Do you suppose they will be able to provide fresh vegetables for the entire trip?"

The edge of the sun was breaking evenly over the eastern horizon. Winter Hall, enjoying the warm breeze of the Pacific morning, was suddenly aware of a presence at his elbow. He turned to find Dragomiloff staring off into the distance.

"Good morning!" Hall smiled. "Did you sleep well?"

Dragomiloff was forced to return the smile.

"As well as could be expected," was his dry reply.

"When I find it difficult to drop off to sleep," Hall offered, "I usually walk the deck. I find that exercise aids me in falling asleep."

"It was certainly not lack of exercise." Dragomiloff suddenly swung his gaze fully upon the tall, handsome young man at his side. "I had a visitor last night before the ship sailed."

Memory returned to Hall like a blow.

"Gray! He was to investigate this ship!"

"Yes. Gray dropped in to see me."

"Is he aboard?" Hall glanced about; his pleasant smile had disappeared.

"No. He did not sail with us. He remained."

Hall stared at the small sandy-haired man beside him with growing comprehension.

"You killed him!"

"Yes, I killed him. I was forced to."

Hall turned back to his contemplation of the sunrise. A sternness had settled over his strong face.

"You say you were forced to. Do I recognize in this admission a change in your beliefs?"

"No." Dragomiloff shook his head. "Although all beliefs must be amenable to change if thinking man is to merit his ability to reason. I say forced to, because Gray was my friend. In a way you might say he was my protégé. It was in following my teachings that he attempted my life. It was in recognition of the purity of his motives that I took his."

Hall sighed wearily.

"No, you have not changed. Tell me, when will this madness end?"

"Madness?" Dragomiloff shrugged his shoulders. "Define your terms. What is sanity? To allow those to live whose course of action leads to the taking of innocent lives? At times, thousands of innocent lives?"

"You certainly cannot be referring to John Gray!"

"I am not. I am merely justifying the basis of my teachings, which John Gray believed in, and which you choose to call madness."

Hall stared at the other hopelessly.

"But you have already admitted the fallacy of that philosophy. Man cannot judge; he can only be judged. And not by the individual. Only by the group."

"True. It was on this basis that you convinced me that the aims of the Assassination Bureau were unworthy. Or possibly a better word would be 'premature.' For the Bureau itself, you must remember, is a group, representative of society itself. Picture a Bureau, if you would, encompassing all mankind. Then the arguments you used to convince me would no longer be valid. But no matter. In any event, you did convince me, and I did undertake the task of having myself assassinated. Unfortunately, the very perfection of the organization has worked against me."

"Perfection!" Hall cried in exasperation. "How can you use that word? They have failed to kill you in at least six or eight attempts!"

"That failure is proof of the perfection," Dragomiloff stated gravely. "I see you do not understand. Failures are calculable; for the Bureau contains within it certain checks and balances. The failures prove the rightness of these checks and balances."

Hall stared at the small man at his side in amazement.

"You are unbelievable! Tell me, when will this—very well, I shall not use the word 'madness'—when will this adventure, then, end?"

To his surprise Dragomiloff smiled in quite a friendly manner.

"I like that word 'adventure.' All life is an adventure, but we do not appreciate it until life itself is in jeopardy. When will it end? When we end, I suppose. When our brains cease to function; when we join the worms and the non-thinkers. In my particular case," he continued, noting Hall's barely concealed impatience, "at the end of a period of one year from the time of my original instructions to Haas."

"And that time is well along. In less than three months your contract will have expired. What then?"

To his surprise Dragomiloff's smile suddenly faded.

"I do not know. I cannot believe that the organization I have built up so painstakingly will allow me to live the full period. That would be a negation of its perfection."

"But certainly you do not want them to succeed?"

Dragomiloff clasped his hands tightly. His face was frowning and serious.

"I do not know. It is something that has been bothering me more and more as the weeks and months have passed."

"You are an amazing person! In what way has it been bothering you?"

The small light-haired man faced his larger companion.

"I am not sure that I wish to be saved by the expiration of a time limit. Time should be the master of people, and not the servant. Time, you see, is the one perfect machine, whose gears are set by the stars, whose hands are controlled by the infinite. I have also built a perfect machine, the Bureau. But the Bureau must depend upon itself to demonstrate that perfection. It must not be saved from its shortcomings by the inexorable function of another, and greater, machine."

"But yet you are attempting to take advantage of the time element for your own salvation," Hall pointed out, intrigued as always by the workings of the other's mind.

"I am human," Dragomiloff replied sadly. "Possibly, in the long run, this may prove to be the fatal weakness of my philosophy."

Without further comment he turned and walked slowly and heavily to the doors leading to the inner parts of the ship. Hall stared after the man a moment, and then felt his arm touched from the other side. He swung about to face Grunya.

"What have you been saying to my father?" she demanded. "He looked quite shaken."

"It is what your father has been saying to himself," Hall replied. He took her arm and they began strolling along the deck. "There is an instinct within each of us to fight to retain life. But there is also within each of us a hidden death-wish, which uses many excuses for justification. We have yet to see which dominates in the life of your strange father."

"Or in his death," she murmured, and clung fiercely to the protective arm of her loved one.

16

The days aboard the *Eastern Clipper* passed swiftly and pleasantly. Grunya basked each day in the warm sun, lying in her deck-chair, and acquired a deep tan, as did Hall. Dragomiloff, however, although spending an equal number of hours on the sun-swept deck, seemed immune to the power of the burning rays and remained as pale as ever. Hall and Dragomiloff seemed to have declared a moratorium on philosophical discussion; their talk now ran more to the schools of bonito and albacore that often played in the wake behind the ship, or to the excellent cuisine served aboard, or even at times to their respective deck-tennis scores.

And then one morning, as if it had never been, the trip was over. They awoke this day and came on deck to find themselves in the shadow of towering Diamond Head at the entrance to the island of Oahu, with the port city of Honolulu lying white and glistening in the background. Small canoes with lei-laden natives were already racing towards the ship. Below, in the bowels of the giant liner, stokers were leaning quietly upon their blackened shovels; the great engines had slowed and the ship was barely making way.

"Beautiful!" Grunya murmured, and turned to Hall. "Is it not beautiful, Winter?"

"Almost as beautiful as you are," Hall replied jocularly, and turned to Dragomiloff. "Ten weeks," he said lightly. "In just ten weeks, sir, our relationship will change. You shall become my father-in-law."

"And no longer your friend?" Dragomiloff laughed.

"Always my friend." Hall frowned slightly. "By the way, what are your plans now? Do you think the other members of the Bureau will follow you here?"

Dragomiloff's smile did not lessen in the least.

"Follow me? They are here now. Or most of them. They would leave at least one on the mainland, of course."

"But how could they arrive sooner than we?"

"By faster ship. I would judge they took the *Oriental Star* the afternoon after we sailed. The discovery of Gray's body would tell them our ship, and hence our destination. They will have docked last evening. They will be on hand when we disembark, do not fear."

"But how can you be so sure?" Grunya demanded.

"By placing myself in their position and calculating what I would do under the same circumstances. No, my dear, I am not wrong. They will be on hand to greet me."

Grunya reached over to grasp his arm, fear growing in her eyes.

"But, Father, what will you do?"

"Do not worry, my dear. I shall not fall victim to them, if that is what you fear. Now pay close heed: several days before sailing I sent a letter on the mail packet making reservations for the two of you at the Queen Anne Inn. There will also be a car and driver available whenever you wish. I myself will not be able to join you, but as soon as I am settled you shall hear from me."

"For the two of us?" Hall was surprised. "But you did not even know I would be coming!"

Dragomiloff smiled broadly.

"I said I always put myself in the other fellow's boots. In your place I would never allow a girl as beautiful as my Grunya to escape me. My dear Hall, I knew you would be aboard this ship."

He turned back to the rail. The native-filled canoes were now bobbing alongside the ship; young boys dressed only in the native *molo* were diving for coins flung by the passengers into the clear water of the harbor entrance. The white buildings along the quay reflected back the morning sun. The giant liner stopped; a slim cruiser flashed from shore carrying the pilot and the Chinese porters who would take off the luggage.

A loud hoot broke the silence as the ship's whistle announced their proud arrival. The pilot boat slipped alongside and the officials, neat in their peaked caps and white shorts, clambered aboard. They were followed by a string of blue-clad, pig-tailed porters who scampered up the Jacob's ladder, their sloping straw hats bobbing in unison, and disappeared into the inner passageway.

Dragomiloff turned to the other two.

"If you will pardon me, I must finish my packing," he said lightly, and with a wave disappeared into the interior of the ship.

The pilot appeared on the bridge and the *Eastern Clipper's* engines began to rumble, changing to a higher pitch as the ship proceeded landwards.

"We had best get below and see to our luggage," Hall remarked.

"Oh, Winter, must we so soon? This is so lovely! See how the mountains seem to sweep up from the city. The clouds are like puff-balls hanging over the peaks!" She paused and the animation died upon her face. "Winter; what will Father do?"

"I should not worry about your father, dear. They may not be here. And even if they are, it is doubtful that they would attempt anything in this crowd. Come."

They went below as the steamer edged closer to the pier. Lines were cast ashore and willing hands linked them to stanchions set in the dock. The ship's winches began turning, winding in the cable, pulling the liner into position along the dock. A band broke into music, playing the famous "Aloha." Screams of recognition broke out as passengers and friends found each other in the crowd; handkerchiefs were waved frantically. The gangplank edged downwards; the band played louder.

Hall, returning to deck after assigning his luggage to a porter, came to stand at the rail staring down at the animated faces strung out behind the railing below. Suddenly he came erect with a start; staring him in the eye was Starkington!

The head of the Chicago branch of the Bureau smiled delightedly and waved his hand. Hall's glance slid along the upturned faces and stopped at another. Hanover was also there, closer to the exit. The rest, Hall was sure, were placed at equally strategic positions.

The gangplank fell into place and the barriers were dropped. Friends and passengers swarmed up and down the gangplank, pushing past heavily laden porters struggling down, swaying perilously beneath their loads. Starkington was mounting the gangplank, shoving his way through the throng. Hall came forward to meet him.

Starkington was smiling happily.

"Hello, Hall! It's nice to see you. How have you been?"

"Starkington! You must not do this thing!"

Starkington raised his eyebrows.

"Must not do what thing? Must not keep our sacred word? Must not remain true to a promise? A commitment?" His smile remained, but the eyes behind the smile were deadly serious. They swung over Hall's shoulder, searching the face of each passenger surging towards the gangplank. "He has no escape this time, Hall. Lucoville came aboard with the pilot boat; he is below at this moment. Hanover is guarding the dock. The Chief made a grave mistake to corner himself in this manner."

Hall gritted his teeth.

"I shall not permit it. I shall speak to the authorities."

"You will speak to no one." Starkington's tone was pedantic; he might have been a professor explaining some obvious point to a rather dull student. "You have given your word of honor. To the Chief himself, as well as to all of us. You did not speak to the authorities before, and you will not speak to them now . . ."

He broke off as a Chinese porter, burdened beneath a mountain of suitcases, stumbled into him with a sing-song excuse. Lucoville appeared at their side. He smiled happily at the sight of Hall.

"Hall! This is a pleasure. How was the trip? Did you enjoy it? Tell me," he continued, lowering his voice, "how were the vegetables aboard this ship? For the return voyage I should prefer a cuisine more in keeping with my tastes. The *Oriental Star* was pitifully short on both vegetables and fruit. Meat, and more meat! I suppose they thought they were doing the passengers a favor . . ."

He seemed to realize that Starkington was waiting, for he dropped the subject and turned to the other.

"Dragomiloff is below. He booked cabin No. 31 under a different name; I have placed an outside latch on the cabin to prevent his escape. However, there is still the porthole . . ."

"Hanover is watching for that." He turned to the white face of Hall beside him. "Hadn't you better go ashore, Hall? Believe me, there is nothing you can do to prevent this."

"I shall remain," Hall exclaimed, and then wheeled as a hand clutched his arm convulsively. "Grunya! Grunya, my dear!"

"Winter!" she cried, and faced Starkington with burning eyes. "What are you doing here? You shall not harm my father!"

"We have discussed this before," Starkington replied smoothly. "You are familiar with our mission, and you are also familiar with your father's instructions. I would suggest, Miss Dragomiloff, that you go ashore. There is nothing you can do."

"Go ashore?" Suddenly she lifted her head in resolution. "Yes, I shall go ashore! And I shall return with the police! I do not care what my father's instructions were; you shall not kill him!" She swung to Hall, her eyes flashing. "And you! You stand there! What kind of a man are you? You are worse than these madmen, for they believe themselves right, while you know they are wrong. And yet you make no move!"

She tore her arm loose from Hall's grip and ran for the gangplank, pushing her way through the thinning crowd. Starkington looked after her, nodding his head sagely.

"You have made a very good choice, Hall. She is a spirited girl. Ah, well, I'm afraid our schedule must be accelerated a bit. I had hoped to wait until the ship was deserted. However, most of the passengers seem to have left. Are you coming?"

This last was said in such a polite voice that Hall could scarcely believe he was being invited to witness the execution of a man, and that man Grunya's father. Starkington smiled at him quite congenially and took his arm.

Hall walked beside the other as if in a dream. It was not believable! One might think he was merely being taken to visit a friend for an afternoon's game of whist! Beside him as they descended the broad carpeted staircase Starkington was chattering quite pleasantly.

"Travel by ship is really delightful, don't you think? We all enjoyed it very much. Lucoville here, of course, constantly complained about the food, but . . . Ah, here we are."

He bent and listened at the door. Faint sounds could be heard from within. He removed the mechanism Lucoville had placed upon the latch and turned to the others.

"Lucoville, stand to that side. Hall, I would suggest you leave the alcove. The Chief is certain to be prepared to defend himself, and I should not like to see harm come to you."

"But you may be killed!" Hall cried.

"Assuredly. However, between Lucoville and myself, one of us should be able to complete the assignment. And that is all that counts."

He withdrew a revolver from his pocket and held it in readiness. To his side Lucoville had done the same. Hall stared at the two in awe; neither exhibited the slightest fear. Starkington took a key from his pocket and inserted it in the lock, making no attempt to mask the sound.

"Back, Hall," he commanded, and in the same moment swung the door wide and charged within. At the sight that faced them Starkington paused, mouth agape, while Hall burst into laughter.

There on the bunk, twisting and squirming, lay a Chinese,

stripped to his underwear and lashed to the bunk. His mouth was firmly gagged, and his eyes were flashing with anger. Even as he twisted his head, frantically imploring his discoverers to free him, they could see the ragged edges where his pig-tail had been severed.

"Dragomiloff!" Lucoville gasped. "He must have been one of the porters that passed us!" He sprang for the door, but Starkington's arm barred his way.

"It is too late," he said evenly. "We must begin our search anew."

There was a commotion in the corridor and Grunya appeared, accompanied by several of the island police, night-sticks poised. At the sight of Hall's convulsed shouts of laughter, Grunya paused uncertainly. The determination of her attitude withered in face of that hilarity. Starkington raised his eyebrows politely.

The police took in the scene at once and then, hastening forwards, released the poor Chinese, who immediately broke into a gale of chatter, pointing first to his severed pig-tail, then to his nearly nude body, and then demonstrated with waving arms the means by which he had been overcome and bound. This all was accompanied by a constant barrage of language. The sergeant of police broke in several times to ask questions in the same tongue, and then turned to Starkington sternly.

"Where is the man responsible for this outrage?" he demanded in English.

"I do not know," Starkington avowed. But then his sense of propriety came to his aid. He reached into his pocket and extracted a fistful of notes, stripping several from the top.

"Here," he said in a kindly voice to the still-outraged Chinese. "You have been no less victimized than ourselves. This will partially compensate for your disgrace. But," and his voice changed to encompass deep regret, "I do not know what will compensate for ours!"

17

Two weeks passed before Grunya and Hall received instructions which were to lead to meeting Dragomiloff. The time had been spent in taking advantage of the car and driver to visit the lovely vistas of the tropical city. The driver had appeared at the Queen Anne Inn the morning after their arrival bearing a note which read:

> "My children, This will introduce Chan, an old and trusted employee of S. Constantine & Co. He will drive you where you want and when you want, save for the few errands I shall require of him. Do not ask him any questions, for he will not answer them. I am well and happy, and will contact you when conditions are ripe. My love to my dear Grunya and a firm handclasp to my friend Hall."

There had been no signature, but none was needed. Satisfied that Dragomiloff was safe, they were able to relax. Their time was spent in typical tourist fashion. They swam at Waikiki, and watched the intrepid surf-riders come sweeping down the foaming ridges of the ocean, racing bent-kneed for the palm-lined shore. They strolled the colorful streets of the city, marveling at the many sights. They enjoyed visiting the fish market on King Street with the vendors crying their wares in eight different languages, or sitting beside Kewolo Basin while the Japanese sampans came wallowing in, loaded to the rail with their catch. Chan, imperturbable, offered neither suggestions nor comment; he drove where he was told and nothing more.

Quite often their evenings were joined by Starkington, Hanover, and Lucoville. Grunya, despite herself, could not help but like the three. Their minds and their attitudes reminded her so much of her father. She was secretly ashamed of her scene aboard ship; she felt it had demonstrated a lack of faith in her father. Somehow, her camaraderie with the trio seemed to her partially to compensate for this failing. Too, each day that passed brought the end of the contract closer, and lessened the danger of the Bureau's success.

One evening this time element had arisen in discussion with the three congenial assassins.

"There are less than two months remaining," Hall mentioned as the five sat at dinner. He laughed. "Believe me, I do not object to your passing the days in this pleasant fashion. In fact, it pleases me to see the funds of the Bureau dissipated in this innocuous way. But I am curious. How does it happen that you are not searching for Dragomiloff?"

"But we are searching," Starkington corrected him gently. "In our own manner. And our search will be successful. I cannot, of course, disclose our plan, but this much I can say: he spent two days at Nanakuli, and the following three days at Waianae. Lucoville investigated in one case, and Hanover in the other. But he had already left."

Hall's eyebrows lifted mockingly.

"You did not investigate yourself?"

"No." There was no embarrassment in Starkington's tone. "I was busy keeping an eye on you and Miss Constantine, although I am sure that you know no more about his whereabouts than we do."

He lifted his glass.

"Let us drink a toast. To the end of this business."

"I will be happy to drink to that," Hall remarked evenly. "Though we mean different things."

"It is the difficulty of all language," Starkington admitted with a rueful smile. "Definition."

"It is not a difficulty," Hanover objected. "Definition is the very basis of language. It is the skeleton upon which the sound-forms are hung that make a language."

"You are speaking about the same language," Lucoville stated solemnly, although his eyes were twinkling. "I am sure that Starkington and Hall are speaking about——or at least are speaking——different languages."

"I thought I was speaking, not about language, but about a toast," Starkington corrected mildly. He lifted his glass. "If there are no more interruptions . . ."

But there was one more.

"In my opinion," Grunya said archly, her eyes reflecting her enjoyment of the repartee, "the important point is that each be true to his own definition."

"I agree!" Lucoville cried.

"And I," added Hanover.

"I . . ." Starkington, who had set down his glass, raised it once more. "I . . . am thirsty." With no further ado he drank. With a laugh, the others joined him.

As they strolled homeward in the balmy night air beneath the giant hibiscus that lined their way, Hall took Grunya's hand in his and felt her fingers tighten.

"How could they have known where Father has been?" she inquired worriedly. "Certainly these islands are too large and too numerous for them to have accidentally stumbled upon his trail."

"They are very clever men," Hall replied thoughtfully. "But your father is also clever. I do not think you need worry."

They swung into the large entrance to the hotel. Beyond, in the bougainvillea-covered courtyard, a *luau* was being held and the soft music of guitars could be heard. At their entrance the receptionist moved away from the door where he had been watching the festivities and came forwards. With their keys, Hall received a sealed note; he tore it open and read it as Grunya waited.

"Dear Hall: My haven is ready at last; my haven and my trap. It has taken time but it has been worth it. Go to your rooms and then descend the rear staircase. Chan will be waiting behind the hotel. Your luggage can be picked up later, although where we shall be staying we shall require few of the symbols of so-called civilization."

There was a strange postscript, underlined for emphasis:

"It is vital that your time-piece be exact when you meet me."

Hall thanked the clerk politely and carelessly thrust the note into his pocket. A slight shake of his head discouraged Grunya from asking questions until they were on the upper floor away from prying eyes.

"What can Father mean by a haven and a trap?" Grunya asked anxiously. "Or by his request that your time-piece be exact when we meet?"

But Hall could offer no suggestion. They swiftly packed their suitcases and left them within the confines of their rooms. A telephone call to the island observatory confirmed the accuracy of Hall's pocket-watch, and moments later they had descended the rear staircase and were peering through the darkness of the moonless night.

A deeper shadow delineated the car. They slid into the rear seat while Chan put the automobile into motion. Without lights they crept through the obscure alley until they came upon a cross-street. Chan flicked on the headlamps and swung into the deserted avenue. A mile or so from the beach he turned again, this time into a wide highway, maintaining his speed.

Until now Hall had remained silent. Now he leaned forwards, speaking quietly into the chauffeur's ear.

"Where are we to meet Mr. Constantine?" he asked.

The Chinese shrugged. "My instructions are to take you beyond Nuuanu Pali pass," he said in his clipped but accurate

English. "There we will be met. Beyond this I can tell you nothing."

Hall leaned back; Grunya clasped his hand, her eyes sparkling at the thought of seeing her father once again. The car rode smoothly along the deserted road, its headlamps cutting a wedge in the hazy darkness. Higher and higher they mounted into the hills as the lights of the city grew smaller in the distance below and then finally disappeared. A sharpness sprang into the air. Without warning Chan increased the speed of the car and they were flung back against the seats, the wind rushing against their faces.

"What . . . ?" Hall began.

"The car behind," Chan explained calmly. "It has been following us since we left. Now is the time to increase our lead, I believe."

Hall swung about. Below them, twisting and turning on the winding road, twin head-lamps marked the passage of a vehicle behind. There was sudden bumping as their car left the macadam; a swirl of dust blocked his vision.

"They will have marked our turn-off!" Hall cried.

"Of course," Chan replied smoothly. "My instructions are not to lose them."

He handled the automobile expertly along the winding dirt road. Dust swirled about them; Hall wished they had put the side-curtains in place. They had passed the ridge of the pass and were now descending. As their vehicle made sharp turns Hall could look back and note, higher on the mountain, the twin shafts of light that marked their pursuers.

Without warning Chan applied the brake; both Grunya and Hall were flung forwards. The car came to a stop; the door was thrown wide and a small figure sprang inside. Immediately they were in motion once again, accelerating through the darkness.

"Who . . . ?"

There was a low chuckle.

"Whom did you expect?" Dragomiloff inquired. He leaned

over and flicked on a small lamp set in the back seat of the swaying car. Grunya gasped at his appearance. Dragomiloff was wearing a jersey and trousers, both once white, but now tattered and marked by the brush. On his feet were a pair of stained tennis-shoes. He kissed his daughter fondly and clasped Hall's outstretched hand. Then, switching off the lamp, he leaned back smiling in the darkness.

"How do you like my costume?" he asked. "Away from the large cities there is no need for formal clothing. Once we are settled, we may even assume the native *molo*. Hall and I, that is. Grunya, you shall have your choice of a *muumuu* or a *pa-u*, as you wish."

"Father," Grunya exclaimed. "You should see yourself! You look like a beachcomber! Where is that dear old solemn Uncle Sergius that I used to tickle and fling pillows at?"

"He is dead, my dear," replied Dragomiloff with a twinkle. "Your Mr. Hall killed him with a few quiet thrusts of logic. The second deadliest weapon that I have ever encountered."

"And the deadliest?" Hall inquired.

"You shall see." Dragomiloff turned to his daughter. "Grunya, my dear, you had best sleep. Explanations can wait. We still have several hours until we reach our destination."

Their car continued down the winding road, leading now towards the eastern shore of the island. The clouds had swept away; to the east the first faint strands of dawn began to appear. Hall leaned towards Dragomiloff.

"You know that we are being followed?"

"Of course. We shall allow them to keep us in sight until we pass the village of Haikuloa. From then on there are no more turn-offs and they cannot mistake our destination. After Haikuloa we can go our way."

"I do not understand this." Hall stared at the small man in frowning contemplation. "Are you the hare or the hound in this weird chase?"

"I am both. Throughout life, every man is both. The chase is constant; only a man's control of the elements of the chase determines whether he be hare or hound."

"And you feel that you control these elements?"

"Completely."

"And yet, you know," Hall said, "they knew you were in Nanakuli and Waianae."

"I wished them to. I planted the evidence that led them there. I laid a trail to the west so they would follow when you and Grunya headed east."

He laughed at the expression on Hall's face.

"Logic comes in many degrees, my friend. If I hold a stone in one hand and you guess that hand correctly, the following time I may switch hands. Or I may retain it in the same hand, calculating you might think I would switch. Or I might switch hands on the basis that you would expect me to reason as I did. Or . . ."

"I know," Hall acknowledged. "It is an old theory of the scales of intelligence. But I fail to see how it applies here."

"I shall explain. First, as to how I marked my passage west to Starkington's satisfaction. I simply ordered books in Russian from the largest bookstore in Honolulu with instructions to deliver them to me at certain small villages along the western coast. Starkington and the others know I would not forego my studies under any circumstances. Had I left a less subtle trail he might not have been taken in, but I knew he would consider this an unconscious gesture on my part."

"But he claimed you had actually visited those places!"

"And I did. There is little bait in an empty hook. However, once he felt he had marked me traveling west, I was ready to lead him east. You and Grunya did this excellently; I am sure that you sneaked down the rear steps of the hotel quite dramatically. And I am equally sure that Starkington watched you do so."

Hall stared at the smaller man.

"You are amazing!"

"Thank you." There was no false modesty in the tone. Drago-miloff lapsed into silence.

The car had passed Haikuloa, and Chan was now intent upon losing those in the following car. The car raced along the narrow dirt road. Suddenly the ocean was just below them, spreading out to the horizon and the rising sun. With a swerve Chan swung off into the brush, drove for several hundred yards, and braked. The silence of the early morning surrounded them.

"One other thing . . ." Hall began.

"Hush! They will be passing soon!"

They waited in silence. Moments later the roar of a heavy car came to their ears. It passed their hiding place with a rush and disappeared on the road leading below. Dragomiloff descended from the car with Hall and led the way to the edge of the cliff upon which they had stopped. Below them a line of thatched huts marked a beach village. Dragomiloff pointed into the distance.

"There. Do you see it? That small island off shore? That is our haven."

Hall stared across the narrow expanse of water that separated the island from the shore. The island was quite small, less than a mile in length and something less than half as much in width. Palm trees ringed the white sand beach; on a small hummock in the center lay a large thatched cottage. No sign of life could be discerned.

Dragomiloff's finger shifted.

"That stretch of water between here and the island is called the *Huhu Kai*—the angry sea."

"I have never seen water as calm," Hall stated. "The name appears to be some sort of joke."

"Do not think so. The floor of the ocean between the shore and the island has a very strange configuration." He broke off this line of thought. "You remembered to check the accuracy of your watch?"

"I did. But why . . ."

"Good! What hour do you have now?"

Hall checked his watch.

"Six forty-three."

Dragomiloff made a rapid calculation.

"There is about one hour yet. Well, we can relax for a bit."

But he did not seem to be able to relax. He paced back and forth restlessly, and finally came to stand beside Hall, peering down at the small thatched village beneath them.

"It will take them some time to descend by car; the road is winding and often dangerous." And then, apropos of nothing in their previous conversation, he murmured, "Righteousness. Morality and righteousness. It is all that we have, but it is enough. Do you know, Hall, that the motto of these islands is *Ua mau ke ea o ka aina i ka pono?* It means: 'The life of the land is preserved in righteousness.'"

"You've been here before?"

"Oh, yes; many times. S. Constantine & Co. have been importing from Hawaii for many years. I had hoped . . ." He did not finish the thought but turned to Hall almost fiercely. He seemed to be in the grip of some sudden excitement.

"What is the hour?"

"Seven-oh-three."

"We must start. We shall leave Grunya here with Chan; it is best. Leave your jacket, it will be warm. Come; we go by foot."

Hall turned for one last glance at the sleeping girl curled in a corner of the car. Chan was sitting imperturbably in the front seat, his eyes staring straight ahead. With a sigh the tall young man wheeled and followed Dragomiloff through a narrow passage in the trees.

18

They came silently through the tall grass to the edge of the palm fringe that bordered the white sand. The water beyond was smooth as silk, the tiny wavelets breaking on the shore in little ripples. In the clear air of morning the tiny island stood sharp and white against the green background of the sea. The sun, now well above the horizon, hung like an orange ball in the east.

Hall was panting from the exertion of their descent; Dragomiloff showed no signs of effort. He swung about to his companion, his eyes bright with anticipation.

"The time!" he demanded.

Hall stared at him, breathing deeply.

"Why this constant attention to the hour?"

"The time!" There was urgency in the smaller man's tone. Hall shrugged.

"Seven-thirty-two."

Dragomiloff nodded in satisfaction and peered down the beach. The row of thatched huts was spread out below them. On the sand a line of hollowed-cut canoes was drawn up. The tide was rising, tugging at the canoes. Even as they watched, a native emerged from one of the huts, dragged the outermost canoes higher onto the sand, and disappeared once again into the shadowed doorway.

The car used by their pursuers was stationed before the largest of the huts, its wheels half-buried in the sand. There was no one in sight. Dragomiloff studied the scene with narrowed eyes, a calculating frown upon his face.

"The time!"

"Seven-thirty-four."

The smaller man nodded.

"We must leave in exactly three minutes. When I start to run across the sand, you will follow. We shall launch that small canoe lying closest to us. I will enter and you will push us off. We will paddle for the island." He paused in thought. "I had planned on their being in sight, but no matter. We shall have to make some sort of outcry . . ."

"Outcry?" Hall stared at his companion. "You wish to be caught?"

"I wish to be followed. Wait—all is well."

Starkington had appeared from the large hut, followed by Hanover and Lucoville. They stood scuffing their feet in the sand, speaking with a native who stood tall and majestic in the open doorway of the hut.

"Excellent!" Dragomiloff's eyes were glued upon the trio. "The time?"

"Exactly seven-thirty-seven."

"The hour! Now!"

He dashed from their refuge, his feet light on the brilliant sand. Hall, running hastily behind, almost tripped but recovered himself in time. Dragomiloff had the small canoe in the water; without hesitation he sprang inside. With a heave Hall set them free and swung aboard, his trouser legs dripping from their immersion. Dragomiloff had already grasped a paddle and was sending them shooting across the calm water. Hall lifted a paddle from the bottom of the boat and joined the smaller man in propelling their slight craft across the smooth sea.

There was a loud shout from the trio on shore. They came hurrying to the edge of the water. A moment later they had clambered aboard a larger canoe and were bent to the paddles. The native ran after them, calling something in a loud voice, waving his hands frantically and pointing seawards, but they paid him no heed. Dragomiloff and Hall increased their efforts; their light canoe momentarily widened the gap.

"This is insane!" Hall gasped, the sweat pouring down his face. "They are three! They will be on us long before we reach the island! And even then that barren rock is no refuge!"

Dragomiloff offered no refutation. His strong back bent and straightened as he lifted and lowered his paddle steadily. Behind them the larger canoe was beginning to gain ground; the distance between the two shallow boats was lessening.

Then, suddenly, Dragomiloff ceased paddling and smiled grimly.

"The hour," he asked quietly. "What is the hour?"

Hall paid no attention. His paddle was digging fiercely into the smooth sea.

"The hour," Dragomiloff insisted calmly.

With a muffled curse Hall threw down his paddle.

"Then let them have you!" he cried in exasperation. He dug into his pocket. "You and your 'what is the hour'! It is seven-forty-one!"

And at that moment there was a slight tremor that ran through their canoe. It was as if some giant hand had nudged it gently. Hall looked up in surprise; the tremor was repeated. Dragomiloff was leaning forwards intently, his hands loose in his lap, staring in the direction of the mainland. Hall swung about and viewed with amazement the sight behind him.

The canoe in pursuit had ceased to make headway. Despite the power of the paddle-strokes of its occupants it remained fixed, as if painted upon the broad ocean. Then, slowly, it began to swing away in a wide circle, a light wake behind it. The trio in the canoe dug more desperately with their paddles, but to no avail. Hall stared. Dragomiloff sat relaxed, viewing the sight with graven face.

On all sides of the restricted arena upon which this drama was being played, the sea remained calm. But in the center, less than four hundred yards from where they lay rocking gently on the bosom of the ocean, the great forces of nature were at work. Slowly the shining waters increased their colossal sweep; the rip-

ples on the surface took on a circular shape. The large canoe
rode the current evenly, hugging the rim of the circle tightly;
the Lilliputian efforts of the paddlers were lost against that vast
array of strength.

The motion of the sea increased. It circled with ever-
increasing velocity. Before Hall's horrified eyes the smooth surface began slowly to dip towards the center, to begin the
formation of a gigantic flat cone with smooth, shining sides. The
canoe coasted free along the green walls, tilted but locked in
place by the giant centrifugal force. The occupants had ceased
paddling; their hands were fastened to the sides of the vessel
while they watched their certain death approach. One paddle
suddenly slipped from the canoe; it accompanied their dizzying
path, lying flat and rigid upon the firm waters at their side.

Hall turned to Dragomiloff in wrath.

"You are a devil!" he cried.

But the other merely continued to watch the frightful scene
with no expression at all upon his face.

"The tide," he murmured, as if to himself. "It is the tide.
What force can compare with the power of nature!"

Hall swung back to the dreadful sight, his jaws clenched.

Deeper and deeper the cone pitched, faster and faster the glassy
walls rushed around, the canoe held fixedly against the glistening
slope. Hall's eyes raised momentarily to the cliff above the village.
The sun, reflected from some heliographic point, located some
part of their automobile. For one brief instant he wondered if
Grunya were watching; then his eyes were drawn back to the
sight before him.

The faces of the three were clearly visible. No fear appeared,
nor did they cry out. They seemed to be discussing something
in an animated fashion; probably, Hall thought with wonder,
the mysteries of the death they would so soon encounter, or the
beauty of the trap into which they had fallen.

The vortex deepened. A sound seemed to come from the
depths of the racing cone, a tortured sound, the sound of rushing

water. The canoe was spinning at an incredible rate. Then it suddenly seemed to slip lower on the burnished slope, to be seeking the oblivion of the depths of its own will. Hall cried out unconsciously. But the slim vessel held, lower in the pit of speeding water, whirling madly. Swifter and swifter it fled along the green shining walls. Hall felt his sight sucked into the abyss before him; his hands were white on the sides of their rocking canoe.

Starkington raised a hand in a brave salute; his head lifted with a smile in their direction. Instantly he was thrown from the canoe. His body raced alongside the small craft, spread-eagled upon the hard water. Then, before Hall's eyes, it slid into the center of the vortex and disappeared.

Hall swung about, facing Dragomiloff.

"You are a devil!" he whispered.

Dragomiloff paid no attention. His eyes were fixed pensively upon the maelstrom. Hall turned back, unable to keep his eyes from the gruesome sight before them.

The large canoe had slipped lower along the sides of the whirling death. Lucoville's mouth was open; he appeared to be shouting some triumphant greeting to the fate that was reaching out with damp fingers to gather them in. Hanover sat calmly.

The boat slid the last few feet; the bow touched the vortex. With a shriek of rending wood the canoe twisted in the air and then disappeared, sucked into the oily maw, crushed by the enormous forces pressing in upon it. Its two occupants were still seated bravely within; they seemed to swirl into the air and then were swallowed by the voracious sea.

The growling of the rushing ocean began to abate, as if sated by this sacrifice of flesh given it. Slowly the huge cone flattened; the vortex rose evenly as the sides assumed horizontal shape. A low wave traveled from the calming waters, rocking their canoe gently, reminding them of their salvation. Hall shuddered.

Behind him there was a stirring.

"We had best return now." Dragomiloff's tone was even.

Hall stared at his companion with loathing.

"You killed them! As surely as if you had struck them down with a knife or a gun!"

"Killed them? Yes. You wished them killed, did you not? You wanted the Assassination Bureau wiped out."

"I wanted them disbanded! I wanted them to cease their activities!"

"One cannot disband ideas. Convictions." His voice was cold. His eyes roamed the empty sea where the large canoe had been sucked into eternity. Sadness entered his tone. "They were my friends."

"Friends!"

"Yes." Dragomiloff picked up his paddle and set it in the water. "We had best return now."

Hall sighed and dipped his paddle into the sea. The canoe moved sluggishly and then gained speed. They passed over the spot where Starkington and the others had met death. Dragomiloff paused for one brief moment, as if in salute to the lost members of the Bureau.

"We shall have to cable Haas," he remarked slowly, and resumed the even rhythm of his paddling.

19

Haas, in San Francisco, waited impatiently for word from the three who had sailed in pursuit of the ex-Chief of the Assassination Bureau. The days passed swiftly, each day bringing closer the end of the compact. Then, at long last, a letter arrived via the mail packet.

"Dear Haas:

"I can see you pacing your room, muttering to yourself in Greek and Hebrew, wondering if we have fallen victim to the lazy charm of this beautiful island. Or if we have fallen victim to D. You can relax; we have done neither.

"But the task has not been easy. D. laid a very neat trail to the west; we are convinced his true flight will be to the east. We are watching his daughter and Hall carefully. The first move they make in this direction will place us on the scent.

"We realize that time is running out, but do not fear. The Bureau has never failed and will not fail now. You can expect a coded cable any day.

"By the way, some incidental intelligence: D. has also used the name Constantine in his travels. We discovered this when we located him aboard the *Eastern Clipper*. Yes, he escaped. When we get together, after this is all over, we will tell you the whole story.

                                                      "Starkington.

"P.S. Lucoville has fallen in love with *poi*, an unpalatable
      mess made from taro root. We shall have even

greater trouble with him and his diet once we return."

Haas laid down the letter with a frown. The mail packet had sailed from Honolulu nine days earlier; certainly there should have been a cable from Starkington by this time. The trio had been in Hawaii nearly a month; less than six weeks remained to complete the assignment. He picked up the letter again, studying it carefully.

Constantine, eh? It rang some faint bell. There was a large export and import firm with that name. They had offices in New York, he knew; possibly they also had offices in Honolulu. He sat in the quiet of the room, the letter dangling from his fingers, while his tremendous brain calculated all of the possibilities.

In sudden resolve he arose. If there were no cable within the next two days he would catch the first steamer to the islands. And in the meantime he would prepare himself, for there would be precious little time once he arrived there. Folding the letter, he slipped it into his pocket and left the room.

His first stop was at the public library. A willing librarian furnished him with a large map of the Hawaiian Islands, and he spread it out upon a table and hunched over it, studying the details of Oahu with care. The trail had been to the west; his finger traced a spidery line that ran along the coast from Honolulu through Nanakuli and Waianae to a small finger of land marked Kaena Point. He nodded. That had been the false trail; Starkington would make no mistake on that score.

The roads to the east were more complex. Some ran over Nuuanu Pali pass and ended in the bush, or meandered down to unnamed beaches. Another thin line marked a road running up and back of Diamond Head, and then coming to the coast at a curved spit marked Mokapu Point. He pushed aside the map and leaned back, thinking.

He tried to put himself in Dragomiloff's place. Why remain

on Oahu? Why not leave for one of the many islands like Niihau or Kauai that spread out to the west; some deserted, some so sparsely inhabited as to make discovery virtually impossible in the little time left to the Bureau? Why remain on the one island that offered the greatest possibility for discovery?

Only, of course, if discovery were desired. He sat up, his brain racing. And why would discovery be desired? Only for a trap! His eye flashed once again to the map before him, but it told him nothing. He knew too little of the terrain. He leaned back once more, employing his giant intelligence.

A trap to catch three people with certainty was difficult. An accident? Too uncertain; one might always remain alive. An ambush? Almost impossible against three trained men such as Starkington, Hanover, and Lucoville. If he were Dragomiloff, faced with the problem, in what manner would he attempt to resolve it?

Not on land. There was always cover available; the conditions were never certain. For one man, yes; but never three. If he were Dragomiloff he would set his trap on the sea, where escape and cover were unavailable. He bent over the large map once again, his heart beating faster.

The eastern coast wound about tenuously, marked by little coves and scattered offshore islands. An island? Possibly. But again there would be the problem of possible cover, although escape would be more difficult. No; it would be the sea. But how do you trap three men on the barren sea? Three men of extraordinary intelligence, each highly trained in assassination, and also in self-protection?

He sighed and folded the map. Further investigation was necessary. He returned the chart to the librarian, thanking her, and left the cool building. One additional possibility occurred to him and he turned his steps in the direction of the Court House.

The clerk of land records nodded pleasantly.

"Yes," he said. "We do have copies of land transactions in

Hawaii. That is, if they are more than six months old. It takes that long to have them registered and filed here." He peered at the thin, intense man facing him. "What would the purchaser's name be, please?"

"Constantine," Haas replied. "S. Constantine & Co."

"The importers? If you will wait one moment . . ."

Haas stared through the dusty window facing the Bay and the constant passage of small and large ships in the distance, but he saw none of this. In his mind's eye he saw a beach, and a boat—no, two boats—bobbing on the ocean off the shore. In one boat Dragomiloff sat quietly, while the other contained Starkington and the others. They remained there, fixed upon his mind, while he searched the scene for some indication of the trap, some means to explain why Dragomiloff was luring them there.

The clerk returned.

"Here we are, sir. S. Constantine & Co. purchased an office block on King Street in 1906. Five years ago. The details are all here, if you would care to examine them."

Haas shook his head.

"No. I am speaking about another land purchase. More recent. On the eastern coast . . ." He hesitated, and suddenly the picture became clear. Suddenly he was sure. Dragomiloff had been planning this coup since the very first day. He straightened, speaking more positively. "The land was bought between ten and eleven months ago."

The clerk disappeared into his files once again. This time when he returned Haas could not repress a small smile of triumph, for again the clerk was carrying a folder.

"I think this is what you are looking for, sir. But the purchase was not effected by the company. It was made in the name of Sergius Constantine, and comprises a small island off the eastern coast of Oahu."

Haas read the details swiftly. His magnificent memory, recalling the chart of the coastline with perfect clarity, instantly located the small island. Thanking the clerk, he left, his footsteps faster, his mind flying as he reviewed the many possibilities.

There could be no doubt that it was a trap, planned for months, and now in the process of execution. The victims had not been known; fate had selected them. He must send a cable at once; Starkington would need to be warned.

He turned into his hotel, forming the words for the telegram in his mind, picturing his code-book lying in his suitcase hidden beneath his shirts. With his key he was handed a small envelope. He slit it open as he walked towards the stairway, and then stopped short. The message was brief and conclusive:

"Haas: Regret to inform you that Starkington, Hanover, and Lucoville died as the result of an unfortunate boating accident. Knew you would want to know. Hall."

For a moment he remained, his fingers grasping the cable tightly as his mind encompassed the disaster. Too late! No time now for warnings; little time for anything. He must take the first boat. The first boat was—the *Amberly,* sailing at dusk. He would need to go to their offices to arrange passage; they were just a few blocks away.

He rushed to the door and into the street, jostling people as he forced his way through the noon-day crowd. Poor Starkington, he had always liked him so much! Hanover, gentle and scholarly, always so excited at the thought of wrong-doing in this naughty world! And Lucoville; he would never again grouse over his food!

The shipping offices were there across the street. Without looking he sprang into the pavement, never noting the huge brewery wagon bearing down upon him. There was a scream from someone along the sidewalk; a startled curse from the driver pulling madly and vainly on the reins. The twin span of grays, frightened by the apparition of the small figure before them, and frenzied by the violent tug of the bit, lashed out wildly. Haas fell beneath the flailing hooves, his last thoughts a recognition of unbearable pain, and the wonder that he should die so far from the palm-fringed beach and the end of his quest.

By mutual consent it was agreed to pass the final days of the fateful year upon the island. Here Dragomiloff, Grunya, and Hall lived in simple fashion, doing their own cooking, drawing their own water, finding their food in the sea as the natives before them had done for years. Surprisingly, they found it pleasant, a relaxing change from the flurry of their lives upon the mainland. But each knew it to be an escape from their problems, and one which could last but a short time.

To his own amazement, Hall found his liking for Dragomiloff returning daily, despite the frightful recollection of Starkington's death. The memory was fading; it slid further into the recesses of his mind until it appeared as a remembered scene from a book long since read, or a panel of a mural viewed in some obscure gallery long forgotten.

Dragomiloff never shirked his share of the chores, nor did he attempt by reason of his position or his age to direct or command. He was always ready with a helping hand at the fishing and the cooking, and the evenness of his temper often led Hall to wonder if the dreadful scene of the whirlpool had actually existed. Yet daily, as the calendar flew, the small man kept more and more to himself. He sat at meals silent and increasingly thoughtful; the tasks he selected were now those suitable to one person. And daily he spent more and more time along the beach, staring across the empty expanse of the sea towards the mainland, as if waiting.

It was in the late afternoon of the penultimate day that he approached Hall, who was crouching in the surf sifting the shallows for the succulent crabs that hid there. His face was taut, although his voice remained even.

"Hall, you are certain that you cabled to Haas?"

Hall looked up, surprised.

"Of course. Why do you ask?"

"I cannot imagine why he has not come."

"Possibly some circumstance beyond his control." Hall stared at his companion. "You know, he is the last of the Assassination Bureau."

Dragomiloff's face was expressionless as he contemplated the brown face of the crouching man.

"Except for me, of course," he stated quietly, and turned in the direction of the hut.

Hall's eyes followed Dragomiloff's figure for a moment and then, with a shrug, he returned to his crabbing. When the small wicker basket was sufficiently full to insure a good evening meal he straightened up, rubbing the cramped muscles of his back. We are all on edge, but there is but one last day, he thought with satisfaction, and then frowned. There was no doubt but that he would miss the island.

The sun was sinking into the green hills of the mainland as he came back to the hut. He placed the basket of squirming crabs in the small kitchen and padded through into the living room. Grunya was bent in deep conversation with her father; they both stopped short as soon as he entered. It was evident they did not wish to be disturbed. Feeling a bit hurt, Hall left the scene abruptly and walked down to the beach. Secrets? he thought a bit bitterly as he tramped the damp sand. Secrets at this late stage?

It was dark when he returned. Dragomiloff was in his room, bent over his writing table, his lamp casting the shadow of his profile sharply against the thatched wall. Grunya was sitting by a small lamp weaving a small mat from palm-fronds. Hall dropped into a chair opposite her and watched the play of her strong hands silently for a few moments. Her usual smile at sight of him was missing.

"Grunya."

She looked up inquiringly, her face set.

"Yes, Winter?"

"Grunya." He kept his voice low. "We are at the end of our days here. Soon we shall return to civilization." He hesitated, somewhat frightened by the solemnity of her face. "Will you— still wish to marry me?"

"Of course." Her eyes dropped once again to the work in her lap; her fingers picked up their chore. "I want nothing more than to marry you."

"And your father?"

She looked up, no muscle of her face moving. Not for the first time Hall noted the sharp resemblance to the blond man in the strong, fine lines of her face.

"What about my father?"

"What will he do? The Assassination Bureau will be no more. It was a large part of his life."

"It was all of his life." Then her eyes came up, unfathomable. They slid over Hall's shoulder and stopped. Hall swung about. Dragomiloff had come into the room and was standing quietly. Grunya's eyes came back to Hall. She attempted a smile.

"Winter, we . . . we need water. Would you . . . ?"

"Of course."

He rose, took the bucket, and walked in the direction of the small spring at the northern end of the island. The moon had risen, large and white, and lit his path with dancing shadows from the stirring flowers along the way. His heart was heavy; Grunya's strange sternness—almost coldness—weighed upon him. But then a lighter thought came. Each of us, he thought, has been subject to strain these past few days. Lord knows how I must have appeared to her! Just a few more days and they would find themselves aboard ship, and the captain could marry them. Man and wife! He filled the bucket and started back, whistling softly to himself.

The water butt was in the kitchen. He up-ended the bucket

and poured; water overflowed, washing against his bare feet. The butt had been full. In sudden fear he threw the bucket down and dashed for the living room. Grunya was still working silently, but her cheeks were wet with tears. A sheaf of papers lay upon the table before her, curled and heavy under the lamp.

"Grunya, my dear! What . . ."

She attempted to continue her work but the tears streamed faster and faster until she flung the weaving from her and fell into his waiting arms.

"Oh, Winter . . . !"

"What is it? What is it, my darling?" Sudden suspicion came to him and he turned in the direction of Dragomiloff's room. The room was dark, but the moonlight, streaming in at the open window, fell across the empty bed. He sprang for the door, but Grunya clutched his arm.

"No! You must not! Read this!"

He paused irresolutely, but the pressure of her hand upon his arm was demanding. Her eyes, raised to his, were filled with tears, but they were filled, also, with determination. Slowly he relaxed and reached for the sheaf of papers. Grunya watched his face as he read, her eyes roving from the broad forehead to the stern jaw, noting the marks of the man who would be her only refuge forever.

"Dear Children:

"I can wait no longer. Haas has not come and my hours are running out.

"You must try and understand me and—as Hall would call it—my madness. I speak now of the action I must take. As head of the Assassination Bureau I accepted a commission; this commission will be fulfilled. The Bureau has never failed and it will not fail now. To do so would negate everything it has ever stood for. I am sure that only death could have prevented Haas from accomplishing his mission, but in our organization the duty always passes to another. As the last member, I must accept it.

"But I do not accept it with sadness. The Bureau was my life, and as it vanishes, so must Ivan Dragomiloff vanish. Nor am I accepting it with shame; pride marks the step I shall take this night. Possibly we were wrong—at one time you, Hall, convinced me that we were. But we were never wrong for the wrong reasons—even in our wrongness there was a rightness.

"That we killed, and that many times, we do not deny. But the terrible thing in killing is not the quantity of victims, but the quality. The death of one Socrates is a far greater crime against humanity than the slaughter of endless hordes of the savages that Genghis Khan led on the brutal rape of Asia; but who truly believes it? The public—were they to know—would scream imprecation down at our Bureau, even as, with the same breath, they glorified to the heavens all forms of thoughtless and needless slaying.

"You doubt me? Walk through the parks of our great cities, and our squares, and our plazas. What monuments do you find to Aristotle? Or to Paine? Or Spinoza? No; these spaces are reserved for the demigods, sword in hand, who led us in all our slaughtering crusades since we raised ourselves from the apes. The late war with Spain will doubtless fill the few remaining spots, both here and in Spain, with horsed heroes, arms raised in bloody salute, commemorating in deathless bronze the victory of violence in the battle for men's minds.

"Yet I allowed myself to be convinced that we were wrong. Why? Because in essence we *were* wrong. The world must come to recognize the joint responsibility for justice; it can no longer remain the aim of a select—and self-selected—few. Even now, the rumblings that come from Europe foreshadow a greater catastrophe than mankind has yet endured, but the salvation must come from a larger morality than even we could offer. It must come from the growing moral fibre of the world itself.

"Yet, one doubt; one question. If that moral fibre be not forthcoming? Then, in some distant age, the Assassination Bureau may well be re-born. For of the deaths that can be laid at our doors, the following may be said: No man died who did not deserve it. No man died whose death did not benefit mankind. It is doubtful if the same will be said of those whose statues rise from the squares after the next 'final' war is fought.

"But time runs out. I ask you, Hall, to guard Grunya. She is the life I bequeath to this earth, the proof that no man, right or wrong, can pass without leaving his mark.

"One last kiss to my Grunya. One final handclasp to you, my friend.

"D."

Hall lifted his eyes from the papers between his fingers; they sought the beautiful face of his loved one.

"You did not attempt to stop him?"

"No." Her gaze was steady and brave. "All my life he has done everything for me. My slightest wish was granted." Her eyes misted; her mouth quivered with an effort for control. "I love him so much! I had no other means of repaying him."

Hall gathered her in his arms, wonder at her great strength flooding him. Suddenly the strain was too much; she burst into violent tears, clutching his arms with all her force.

"Oh, Winter, was I wrong? Was I wrong? Should I have begged him for his life?"

He held her tightly, soothingly. Through the open doorway his eyes sought the smooth sea reflected brightly in the brilliant moonlight. A shadow crossed his vision, a slight figure in the distance, bent easily over a paddle, moving quietly to the center of the channel to await the *Huhu Kai*. He did not know whether he saw it or imagined it, but suddenly one arm seemed to rise from the dwindling canoe in a happy salute.

"No," he said fiercely, holding her tighter. "No, my darling. You were not wrong."

THE END

[*Jack London's narrative stops on page 109 with the paragraph "Hall, who had sat down, again stood up, moving the wineglass to one side as he rested one hand on the table." At this point, Robert L. Fish's completion of the novel begins.*]

JACK LONDON'S NOTES FOR
THE COMPLETION OF THE BOOK

You "sped the blow" before the truce up. Drago finds this out. Alarm of Breen when he sees the point. "But I can't stop it. Any attempt to stop it will immediately explode it."

Drago: "I'll help you out," Breen grateful.

They prove to Breen that he set it in the truce. "You're right. I almost was guilty of wrong. Disconnect it—I can't. That was the device I mentioned. The beauty of this machine is that it is like a decree of the Bureau. Once set, as it is set, no power on earth can stop it. Automatic locking device. A blacksmith could not now remove the clockwork."

Take it down and throw it in the Bay.

"Friends, lunatics—will you permit this?"

"They can't stop it," Hanover chuckled. "The irrefragable logic of the elements! The irrefragable logic of the elements!"

"Are you going to stay here and be blown up?" Hall demanded angrily.

"Certainly not. But, as Breen says, there is plenty of time. Ten minutes will remove the slowest of us outside the area of destruction. In the meantime consider the marvel of it!"

Hall considers other people.

Breen: "I broke down in my reasoning. That shows fallibility of human reason. But, Hanover, you see no breakdown in the reasoning of the elements. Can't break."

So absorbed, all forgot the flight of time, Drago stood up, and put an affectionate hand on Lucoville's shoulder—near to the neck.

Speaks pleasantly.—swift—spasmodic—hand. Death-touch of Japanese. Caught hat and coat. Slips out—Haas springing like a tiger, collided with servant—crash of dishes.

"Dear friend Lucoville," says Hanover, peering through spectacles. "You will never reply."

The Chief truly had the last word.

———————

Next day's papers—*San Francisco Examiner*—mysterious explosion in Bay—dead fish. No clue.

Drago's message: "Going to Los Angeles. Shall remain some time. Come and get me."

At dinner when Drago had exalted adventure path—they accused him of being a sentimentalist, an Epicurean (sneered).

———————

"Gentlemen!" Hall cried desperately, "I appeal to you as mathematicians. Ethics can be reduced to science. Why give all your lives for his?

Gentlemen, fellow madmen—reflect. Cast this situation in terms of an equation. It is unscientific, irrational. More, it is unmoral. As high ethicists it would be a wanton act, etc."

They debate. They give in.

Drago: "Wisely done. And now, a truce. I believe we are the only group in the United States or the world who so trust." Pulls out watch. "It is 9:30. Let us go and have dinner. 2 hours truce. After that, if nothing is determined or deranged, let the status quo continue.

———————

Hall loses Grunya, who saves Drago, and escapes with him. Then Hall, telegrams, traces them through Mexico, West Indies, Panama, Ecuador—cables big (5 times) sum to Drago, and starts in pursuit.

Arrives; finds them gone. Encounters Haas, and follows him. Sail on same windjammer for Australia. There loses Haas.

Himself, cabling, locates them as headed for Tahiti. Meets them in Tahiti. Marries Grunya. Appearance of Haas.

The three, Drago, Grunya and Hall (married) live in Tahiti until assassins arrive. Then Drago sneaks in cutter for Taiohae.

Drago assures others of his sanity; they're not even insane. They're stupid. They cannot understand the transvaluation of values he has achieved.

On a sandy islet, Dragomiloff manages to blow up the whole group except Haas who is too avidly clever. House mined.

Drago, in Nuka Island, village Taiohae, Marquesas. There is a wrecked cutter and assassin (Haas) is thrown up on beach where Melville escaped nearly a century earlier. While Drago is off exploring Typee Valley on this island, Hall and Grunya play off the assassin Haas, and think are rid of him.

Drago dies triumphantly: Weak, helpless, on Marquesas island, by accident of wreck is discovered by appointed slayer—Haas. Only by accident, however. "In truth I have outwitted organization." Slayer and he discuss way he is to die. Drago has a slow, painless poison. Agrees to take. Takes. Will be an hour in dying. Drago: "Now, let us discuss the wrongness of the organization which must be disbanded."

Grunya and Hall arrive. Schooner lying on and off. They come ashore in whaleboat, in time for his end. After all dead but Haas, Hall cleaned up the affairs of the Bureau. $117,000 was turned over to him. Stored books and furniture of Drago. Sent mute to be caretaker of the bungalow at Edge Moor.

ENDING AS OUTLINED
BY CHARMIAN LONDON

The small yacht sailing, spinnaker winged out, day and night, for many days and nights. The saturnalia of destruction—splendid description of the bonita—by the hundreds of thousands. The great hunting. The miles wide swatch of destruction. The gunies, bosuns, frigate birds, etc., increasing—tens of thousands. All after flying fish. When flying fish come aboard, they, too, rush to catch them. Saturnalia of killing gets on their nerves. Birds break wings against rigging, fall overboard, torn to pieces by bonita and attacked from above by their fluttering kind—frigate birds, bosuns, etc. Native sailors catch bonita to eat raw—as haul in, caught-bonita are attacked by their fellows. Sailors catch a shark—cut it clean open, none of its parts left. Beating heart in a man's hand—shark heaved overboard, swims and swims, snapping with jaws as the bonita hosts flit by in the sun-flooded brine—beating heart shock to Grunya. Finally the madness of the tropic sun, etc. Here begin to shoot birds, fish, etc., with small automatic rifle, and she looks up and applauds. All killed or injured are immediately eaten by others. Once the Irish terrier goes overboard and is torn to pieces by bonita. Once, her scarf, red, struck and dragged down, etc., etc. Nothing can escape.

And so the end, tragic foredoomed, as they go ashore, sharks snap at their oar blades. And on the beach, a school of small fish, discovered, rush upon the beach. They wade ashore through this silvery surf of perished life, and find—Dragomiloff dying.

FOR THE BEST IN PAPERBACKS, LOOK FOR THE 🐧

In every corner of the world, on every subject under the sun, Penguin represents quality and variety—the very best in publishing today.

For complete information about books available from Penguin—including Pelicans, Puffins, Peregrines, and Penguin Classics—and how to order them, write to us at the appropriate address below. Please note that for copyright reasons the selection of books varies from country to country.

In the United Kingdom: For a complete list of books available from Penguin in the U.K., please write to *Dept E.P., Penguin Books Ltd, Harmondsworth, Middlesex, UB7 0DA.*

In the United States: For a complete list of books available from Penguin in the U.S., please write to *Consumer Sales, Penguin USA, P.O. Box 999— Dept. 17109, Bergenfield, New Jersey 07621-0120.* VISA and MasterCard holders call 1-800-253-6476 to order all Penguin titles.

In Canada: For a complete list of books available from Penguin in Canada, please write to *Penguin Books Canada Ltd, 10 Alcorn Avenue, Suite 300, Toronto, Ontario, Canada M4V 3B2.*

In Australia: For a complete list of books available from Penguin in Australia, please write to the *Marketing Department, Penguin Books Ltd, P.O. Box 257, Ringwood, Victoria 3134.*

In New Zealand: For a complete list of books available from Penguin in New Zealand, please write to the *Marketing Department, Penguin Books (NZ) Ltd, Private Bag, Takapuna, Auckland 9.*

In India: For a complete list of books available from Penguin, please write to *Penguin Overseas Ltd, 706 Eros Apartments, 56 Nehru Place, New Delhi, 110019.*

In Holland: For a complete list of books available from Penguin in Holland, please write to *Penguin Books Nederland B.V., Postbus 195, NL-1380AD Weesp, Netherlands.*

In Germany: For a complete list of books available from Penguin, please write to *Penguin Books Ltd, Friedrichstrasse 10-12, D-6000 Frankfurt Main 1, Federal Republic of Germany.*

In Spain: For a complete list of books available from Penguin in Spain, please write to *Longman, Penguin España, Calle San Nicolas 15, E-28013 Madrid, Spain.*

In Japan: For a complete list of books available from Penguin in Japan, please write to *Longman Penguin Japan Co Ltd, Yamaguchi Building, 2-12-9 Kanda Jimbocho, Chiyoda-Ku, Tokyo 101, Japan.*

STILTED, SOPHOMORIC NAVEL-GAZING.
LONDON'S MIND MUST HAVE BEEN GOING.